Published by Samantha Sabian and Arianthem Press

THE DRAGON'S ALLIANCE Vol 5 CHRONICLES OF ARIANTHEM, 2015. FIRST PRINTING.

Office of Publication: Los Angeles, California

What did you think of this book? We love to hear from our readers.

Please email us at: samantha@arianthem.com.

The Dragon's Alliance

The Chronicles of Arianthem V

Samantha Sabian

Arianthem Press

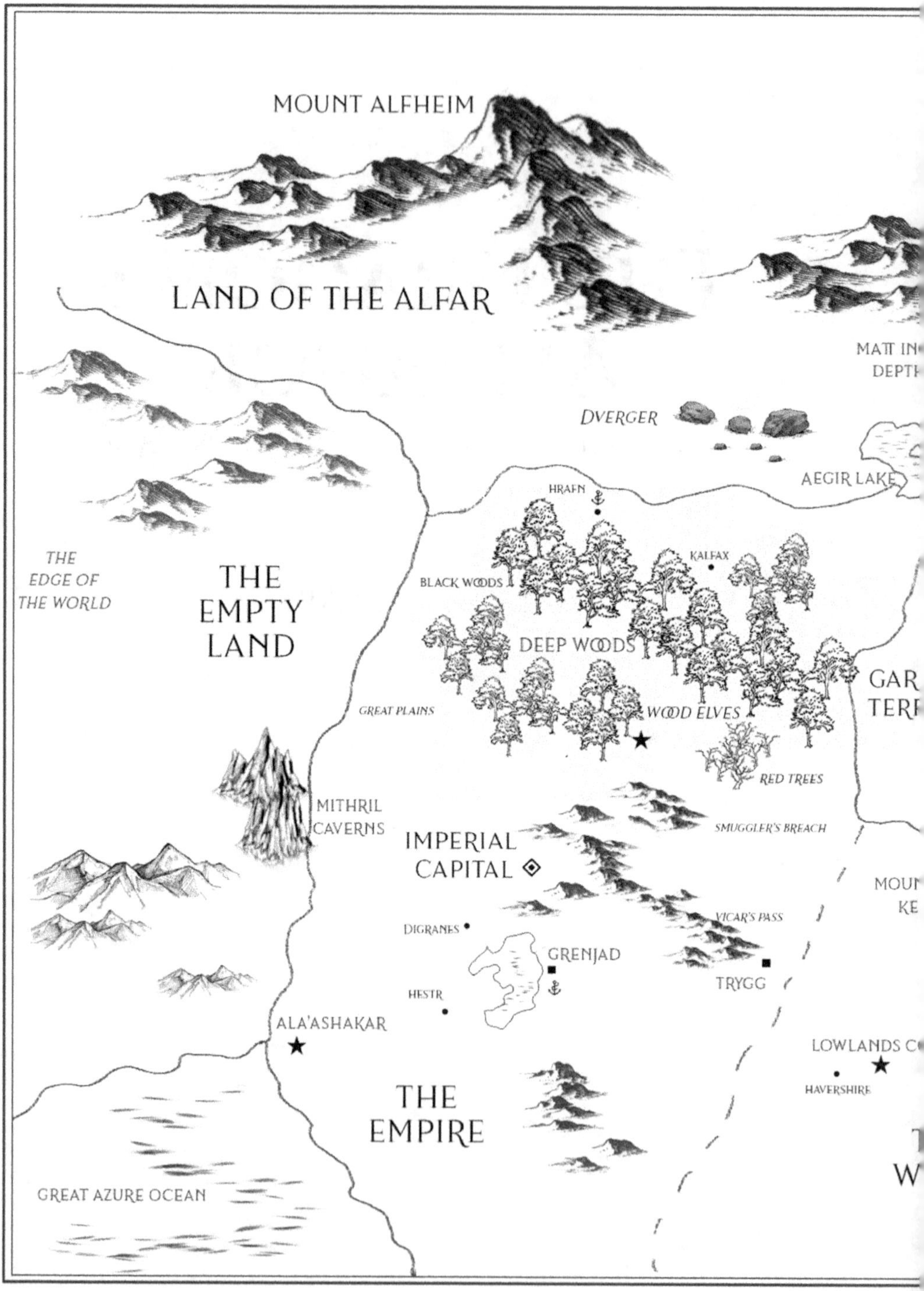
MOUNT ALFHEIM
LAND OF THE ALFAR
DVERGER
AEGIR LAKE
HRAFN
KALFAX
BLACK WOODS
DEEP WOODS
WOOD ELVES
RED TREES
THE EDGE OF THE WORLD
THE EMPTY LAND
GREAT PLAINS
MITHRIL CAVERNS
IMPERIAL CAPITAL
SMUGGLER'S BREACH
VICAR'S PASS
DIGRANES
GRENJAD
TRYGG
HESTR
ALA'ASHAKAR
THE EMPIRE
HAVERSHIRE
GREAT AZURE OCEAN

GONS
KYLAN'S CASTLE
BALDUR'S PEAK
DARBY FALLS
REIST KEEP
DVERGER
NTER
TORY
GUDRID
HALDIS
THE SJOFN ACADEMY
LAND OF THE HA'KAN
N
W
E
S
ARIANTHEM
CIRCA 312 AGW

Chapter 1

The marble terrace was a wonder of architecture, beautifully constructed so that it encircled the Queen's chambers and those of her staff, situated so that it overlooked the palace grounds and the skyline of the Ha'kan capital itself. The terrace was equally shared by the Queen, the High Priestess, the First General, the First Scholar, and any they chose to invite or entertain. For that reason alone, most Ha'kan would glance upward from time to time, hoping to catch a glimpse of their beloved royal staff.

But these days, many would glance up because more often than not, there was an enormous, fiery red dragon perched upon the parapet there, its gleaming gold eyes staring off into the distance, a terrifying protector of the Ha'kan and all within their territory. And sometimes a much smaller figure would join the dragon, one outwardly less imposing, but one as dangerous and equally effective in protecting the Ha'kan. And inevitably, when this second figure appeared, the dragon would disappear into a brilliant flash of yellow light, replaced by an elegant, silver-haired woman in fiery red armor who would take her young lover in her arms.

The morning air was cool and Raine welcomed the warmth of Weynild's embrace. Although Raine wore a silky, full-length robe in the Ha'kan fashion, Weynild could feel the coolness of Raine's skin through the fabric.

"You're still cold."

"Yes," Raine replied, "It's frustrating how slow my energy returns."

As she said this, Raine turned to look out over the Ha'kan capital and beyond. Weynild settled in behind her, pressing her full length against her body and wrapping her arms about her once more. Raine enjoyed the sensation and heat. Her dragon lover was a skilled shapeshifter. Although she could transform herself into almost any form, Weynild chose a human version consistent with her dragon form, older in appearance than most with such an ability would have preferred. But Raine had been attracted to the dragon on first sight, and when she transformed into the older, regal beauty of her human form, Raine was lost to her.

"Most wouldn't have survived Hel's touch, yet you chide yourself because you've not healed in a week."

And it had been only a week. A week since Skye, the young ruler of the Tavinter and beloved friend and ally of the Ha'kan had been attacked by monstrosities from the Underworld. A week since the most powerful of the Ha'kan, including the Princess, the First General, and the First Scholar had sprung to Skye's aid, unfortunately to little avail. A week since Raine had appeared seemingly out of nowhere to do battle with the creatures, warned by the dreams of a powerful mage.

Weynild's golden eyes narrowed and she unconsciously held Raine tighter. A week since Hel had manifested within the Membrane and put her hands and lips upon her lover.

Raine made a small noise and Weynild loosened her grip. "Sorry, my love."

Raine grinned and Weynild was pleased to see her usual irrepressible good humor returning. "You're not hurting me," she said, "but you know your strength arouses me, and that's probably the one thing I'm still not capable of."

Weynild buried her face in Raine's hair. She possessed the strength of a dragon even in human form, so she was one of the few in all Arianthem who was stronger than Raine. She also possessed the legendary lust of the dragons in her human form so their couplings were brutally passionate. Although Weynild had no doubt Raine would survive such passion, at the moment, it most likely would delay her recovery.

"That's been the worst of all this," Raine said, tongue-in-cheek, "that I've had to lie next to you and behave."

"Trust me," Weynild said in that low, throaty tone that Raine so loved. "It's been just as torturous for me. Although I must say, I'm enjoying our time together."

Raine silently agreed. Lately, they had been apart far too much and for far too long for her liking. It was wonderful just to spend the days together in the beauty of the Ha'kan palace, even with so much darkness looming on the horizon.

A stunning woman dressed in the raiment of the Priestess caste approached them on the terrace. She moved with the mesmerizing grace and sensuality befitting the High Priestess of the Ha'kan.

"Astrid," Raine said in greeting, and the High Priestess smiled warmly.

"Good morning, Raine, Talan."

Weynild nodded at the formal recognition. Her true name was Talan'alaith'illaria, Queen of all Dragons, and most in Arianthem used the title as a form of reverence. "And how are you feeling this morning?" Astrid asked, addressing Raine.

"I grow stronger every day," Raine replied, "thank you. The stiffness in my limbs is starting to go away."

"Senta's made a suggestion regarding your recovery," Astrid said. Senta was the imposing First General of the Ha'kan, a strong, handsome woman known for her bravery and skill in battle, and a valued member of Queen Halla's inner circle.

"I welcome Senta's advice," Raine said.

Astrid paused delicately. "Well, it might be something the two of you would like to do together."

This caught Weynild's attention and she turned her glowing amber eyes upon the High Priestess.

"The Ha'kan baths are known for their rejuvenating effect."

Raine's eyes lit up. "The Ha'kan baths!" she exclaimed. "I've heard of this fabled place."

Weynild looked wryly at her mischievous lover. The Ha'kan were a race made up solely of females, non-monogamous and highly sexual by nature. Their culture was built upon sexual relationships and although love was always accompanied by sex, the reverse was only occasionally true. Sex was a soothing, binding, pleasurable experience that permeated the entire society. It was so deeply ingrained within their culture that Astrid's responsibility as High Priestess was to head the Ministry, a branch of their government devoted to the sexual development and well-being of her people.

Needless to say, the stories of the Ha'kan baths were legendary.

Raine was teasing Weynild, but she noticed a look in those gold eyes, a reminisce, a very fond remembrance.

"You," Raine said knowingly, "have been to the baths before."

"Yes, I've been to the Ha'kan baths before."

Astrid was surprised, and her surprise was evident.

"It was long before your time," Weynild explained, "and long before even your great-grandmother's. But as a young dragon, I was known to avail myself of the hospitality of the Ha'kan.

Astrid smiled warmly at the thought.

"And just how much 'hospitality' did you avail yourself of?" Raine asked in mock accusation.

"I assure you," Weynild said, "all of it."

Raine grinned at the thought, and Weynild once again felt her love for the youngster nearly overwhelm her. The "youngster" was centuries older than the High Priestess next to her, but Weynild's age stretched past a millennium, so Raine was indeed young to her. But Raine had such a careless confidence about her it made her nearly incapable of jealousy, which was a good thing as dragons were a lusty lot and the number of Weynild's former lovers rivaled the number of stars in the sky.

Raine, however, had experienced only one lover and the dragon was not quite as careless when it came to her possession. Raine did so little to stoke the fires of jealousy, though, it was an emotion that Weynild rarely felt. And the Ha'kan, as sexual as they were, by their very open nature did not elicit that response.

"And would you deny me the hospitality you yourself enjoyed?" Raine asked, still teasing.

"Of course not," Weynild responded. "You may enjoy the hospitality of the Ha'kan."

"All of it?"

Gold eyes glowered at her. "No," Weynild said emphatically. "Not all of it."

Raine simply laughed and the two walked off hand-in-hand under Astrid's smiling gaze.

Raine wore another robe, this one white and made of soft cotton. It was the Ha'kan garb generally worn to the baths, although once there, many women draped towels about themselves, and some wore nothing at all. Weynild also wore the luxurious robe associated with bathing and it gave her a distinctly different look than the fiery red armor she normally manifested. Manifested, rather than wore, was the proper description because the armor was actually a part of her. But she could remove it with a mental shrug, and often did so to lie skin-to-skin with Raine.

The robe did not, Raine thought with a sideways glance, make her look any less regal or terrifying.

"What?" Weynild asked, her gold eyes coming around with great precision.

"Oh, nothing," Raine said. "Just thinking that you look so marvelous in that robe, this will be difficult."

"Hmm," Weynild said noncommittally. The truth of it was that it would be torture, and really, she could not guarantee her continued abstinence from her love much longer.

The baths were as much a marvel of architecture as the great terrace outside, and perhaps even more so. It was said the ancient dwarves had created the mechanical steam contraptions deep in the earth as repayment for a favor from the ancient Ha'kan. As a result of these mechanical wonders, the room was warm, steamy, and smelled of lavender, juniper, and many other wonderful fragrances. The various pools were different shapes and sizes, some designed for a communal experience, others much smaller and designed for a more intimate experience. Steps flowed down into the water so that the participants could sit on the edge, be partially submerged or relax with the water up to their necks. As always, there were alcoves for various flirtations but most of the intricately tiled room was open. It was lightly attended this morning as most Ha'kan had gone about their daily business.

A lovely woman in the wonder of mature, Ha'kan adulthood flowed toward them. Weynild surmised she was from the Priestess caste based on the warmth and sensuality that emanated from her like warmth and light emanated from the sun.

"My name is Ima," the Priestess said. "I'm Senta's personal therapist. She said you might benefit from some healing work."

"That would be wonderful," Raine said. "If you can work the kinks out of the First General, I'm certain you'll work magic with me."

Ima bowed gracefully in acknowledgement and led them to a space designated for such a purpose. It was a tiled, sunken square with steps leading down to some cushioned tables. The square was bordered by wide, marble ledges with cushions strewn about where Weynild settled comfortably. Bodily shame was a foreign concept to the Ha'kan, and their appreciation of the female form bordered on worship, so it was highly consistent that such an area would not be hidden in a back room but rather set in open theater. Raine followed Ima to one of the tables.

"You may wear the robe if you like, although generally the massage is conducted without clothing."

Raine shrugged. "When in Haldis," she said, referring to the Ha'kan capital, and dropped her robe.

Ima, surrounded with beauty from birth and trained from a young age to be a model of tact and self-control, struggled to maintain her composure. Weynild could not help but notice that the woman strumming the lute in the corner missed several notes as the instrument emitted a discordant mess until it got back on key. And her lover, who stood like a god carved from marble, was as oblivious as always as she went face down on the table in a lithe movement that made the muscles in her arms and back bunch, then relax in glorious repose.

Ima stood for a moment, gathered herself, then went to work. It took all her willpower to concentrate upon the task at hand because the muscles were like steel, but the skin was silky smooth, a heady combination. The shoulders were broad but not manly, the back tapering to slim hips and strong legs. Every muscle was developed and defined and had Raine any extra flesh on her she might have been large. But she had none and instead was a perfect specimen of physicality, a body that had been blessed by the gods at birth, then trained through constant, strenuous activity over centuries.

Weynild glanced up at a figure at her side.

"I'll not stand up there peering around the columns like some schoolgirl," Astrid said, settling in beside Weynild. "I'll come down here and get a front row seat."

Weynild shifted, making room for the High Priestess next to her, welcoming her company. The appreciation of the Ha'kan did not inspire any ire in her. Paradoxically, she found it enjoyable, although it did significantly increase the odds that Raine's recovery would be delayed as there was little doubt she would be pinning that little exhibitionist to her bed before long.

Another figure approached Weynild and she turned as Queen Halla settled in on her other side, also dressed in a white robe. Astrid leaned forward to address the Queen.

"Bathing a bit late this morning?"

Halla paused, then decided equivocation was unnecessary. "No, no," she said without a trace of self-recrimination, "I came for the show."

Weynild smiled at the openness of the two gorgeous women flanking her. It was of infinite enjoyment to sit between the loveliness of the Queen and High Priestess of the Ha'kan while watching her lover murmur with pleasure as hands moved skillfully over her body. She leaned forward and blew out a breath of hot air that whispered over the surface of Raine's skin. The sensation was so pleasurable to Raine she could not control the response and muttered a mild imprecation which she muffled by pressing her face into the sheets.

It did have the desired result, however, and the intricate blue and gold markings that Raine normally kept hidden rose to the surface of her skin. Halla gasped in astonishment. The pattern was beautiful, spread over Raine's back, traveling up over her shoulders, then down her arms and forearms. Ima could not resist and traced the markings with her fingers which elicited another anguished sound from Raine as the markings were actually scars that to this day were hypersensitive. The touch made every part of her alive and she had to keep from squirming in her very pleasant and pronounced discomfort. She had buried her face in the cushions of the table when the heat had flowed over her skin, but now she turned to Weynild.

"If you don't stop this," Raine said through gritted teeth, "the Ha'kan will get to see far more than my markings."

"But then you'll be flat on your back," Weynild said, her tone even drier, "and they won't get to see your pretty little markings at all."

Raine relented. "I would argue," she said off-handedly to Ima, "but 'tis true."

"By the gods, her eyes are beautiful," Astrid murmured as Ima regained her composure and continued her work.

Raine's eyes had turned a deep violet when she looked upon Weynild, another characteristic she kept hidden for very different reasons. Raine was half Scinterian and half Arlanian, two mythic races that had passed into extinction. The Scinterians, once the greatest warriors in all of Arianthem, were first dragon slayers, then fiercely loyal allies to them. Scinterian children acquired the markings in a ceremony designed to inflict such agonizing pain they would never experience worse, and therefore would not fear it.

The Arlanians, on the other hand, were as different from the Scinterians as earth was from sky. A gentle race, dark haired and violet eyed, not fully male or female until adulthood, they were skilled artists and musicians, but had no fighting ability whatsoever. They were blessed with an intense sexual desirability that became a curse when their race was discovered and they were raped into extinction. Wars were fought over the last few survivors, and they considered it a gift they could not reproduce outside their race, embracing extinction rather than the degradation of sexual slavery.

Raine was the improbable, no, impossible progeny from the union of those two races, and the sole survivor of each. Both races were long-lived, and so she had found her perfect mate in the immortal dragon, Talan'alaith'illaria, because it took an Arlanian to satisfy the mythical beast and a Scinterian to survive the act.

"Mmm, yes they are," Weynild agreed in a tone of distraction, one that caused the two Ha'kan women to smile. The dragon was very absorbed at the moment.

"Ima, I think the massage is over," Astrid gently suggested.

Ima glanced up, saw the look on Talan's face, and smiled her agreement.

Raine started to protest. "That seemed a bit short..." She then caught sight of those glowing gold eyes.

"Oh, I see."

The last bit of pleasure was wrung from Raine as she collapsed backward into the soft pillows of her bed. Weynild sat atop her, straddling her, her long limbs pinning Raine's hands above her head, her firm breasts proudly erect, having offered Raine such an astonishing view in their just-finished acrobatics.

"And who is the dragon rider now?" Weynild said, leaning down to kiss Raine's neck, enjoying the saltiness of her skin.

The pun was not lost on Raine. "Yes, yes, I submit the dragon has ridden me very hard."

"Not too hard, I hope," Weynild murmured, still kissing Raine's neck, no contrition in her tone at all.

"Your concern for my well-being is noted."

"It's your fault for being so indestructible," Weynild said, now kissing the other side of her neck. The feel of Weynild's breasts pressing against her skin was wondrous to Raine.

"At least I'm not cold anymore. Perhaps we should've done that a week ago."

"Mmm," Weynild responded. No, Raine's skin was definitely not cold any longer. She released her captive and rolled onto her side, disengaging herself from the Ha'kan contraption Raine wore. Raine released the clasp on the belt and set the device to the side.

"The Ha'kan do make the most marvelous sexual toys," Weynild said. "I shall have to thank the High Priestess for her suggestion."

Raine examined the harness from her prone position. "Skye told me there's an entire guild devoted to the development and manufacture of such devices, a collaboration between Priestesses and Scholars. Can you imagine being the test subject for these experiments?" Raine then frowned a little. "It did please you, didn't it? I was a little distracted with my own pleasure."

Weynild looked upon her lover with fond exasperation. She had been the one on top, taking her pleasure at will and riding her companion so hard it was fortunate she didn't grind her to dust. "I climaxed at least three times," Weynild said, "and that was before that."

Raine turned to where Weynild was nodding. The chair next to the bed had been charred and was now little more than chair-shaped ash. "Ah," Raine said, "a release in more ways than one."

"It's a good thing that most of the Ha'kan palace is stone and tile, otherwise we might burn it to the ground." Weynild propped herself up on her elbow. "I do think you should rest for a while."

"While you do what?" Raine asked, suspicious of her tone.

"I'm going to fly out to the border, see where the Alfar and imperials are, gauge the timing of their arrival."

"They can't be too close. The Tavinter would have reported them."

This was true. Skye's people were forest nomads and excellent scouts. They acted as rangers for the Ha'kan, both in peace and war, and it was an alliance that complemented the strengths of both races. No one would cross into Ha'kan territory without the Tavinter knowing it.

"I could go with you," Raine suggested.

There was an impish quality to the suggestion and Weynild turned her glowing eyes upon the lithe creature in her bed. "I imagine the Alfar would be here before we even reached the edge of the forest."

Dragons were intensely proud, and few mortals ever had the honor of riding aback one. Raine was the exception, not only because she was Weynild's lover but because she was Scinterian, the ancient allies among the few in history who were accorded such an honor. But riding aloft Weynild in dragon form, the sinuous neck between her legs paired with the rhythmic beating of her powerful wings, almost always drove Raine mad with desire. And Weynild, who lived to satisfy her Arlanian, would dive toward the earth to sate that need. Unless urgency demanded, dragon flight with Raine was not always faster than walking.

"I could try and exhibit some self-control," Raine said doubtfully. "Maybe." She paused again. "Okay, not at all."

Weynild gathered her into her arms. "I want you to sleep. I'll be back before you wake."

It was evident Raine was not completely recovered, for she fell asleep in minutes. She moved fitfully when Weynild gently disentangled herself.We ynild wrapped the goose-down comforter about her and then brought the embers in the fireplace to life with merely a breath.

A short time later, the gigantic, magical creature appeared on the parapet of the royal palace. The mighty legs flexed, tendons contracted, and the dragon leaped skyward, the great wings unfurling like the mainsail of a ship. All Ha'kan below stopped what they were doing to watch the magnificent, iridescent drake glide over their capital, then with a great thrust of wings, swoop powerfully toward the open sky.

Raine slept for a few hours and was disappointed to find Weynild had not returned. She was not really surprised, however, as Ha'kan lands were extensive and their border was hundreds of miles away. She did not think the Alfar would be here for weeks. She washed herself in the cool water from a nearby porcelain bowl, then pulled on a pair of breeches, a loose shirt, and yet another elegant robe that had been provided by her hosts.

She pushed through the wood-framed, stained glass doors that bordered the terrace and saw Queen Halla and her staff seated about a table under some fronds shaped into an umbrella. It was spring in the Ha'kan capital, and although the mornings still held a chill, the afternoons were warm. The High Priestess waved for her to join them.

"And how was your massage?" Senta asked as Raine approached.

"Most excellent, First General, thank you for your recommendation," Raine replied, taking the seat offered her.

Queen Halla dabbed at the corner of her mouth with a napkin. It was not Ima who was responsible for the look of contentment on Raine's face.

Gimle, the lovely, willowy First Scholar, spoke up. "I was disappointed I missed it. I would've liked to see your markings."

Astrid turned her knowing, heated gaze upon the First Scholar. "And everything else, of course," Gimle said without hesitation. "But I am fascinated by the markings."

Senta laughed and raised her favored black tea to her lips. She herself had been disappointed she had missed the show.

"You may see them at any time," Raine offered. She extended her forearm to Gimle and pulled up her sleeve. "They're always there. I merely control whether or not they can be seen."

As she said this, she clenched her fist and the beautiful blue and gold pattern rose to the surface. All of the Ha'kan leaned forward with interest.

"May I touch it?" Gimle asked.

"Of course," Raine said, then caught her breath as Gimle brushed her fingers across the surface of her skin. "They're scars," Raine explained, "but somehow they're still sensitive after all these years. Not in a bad way," she added, "not painful."

"How is it you're able to hide them?" Gimle asked. "And your eyes as well?"

"I'm not completely sure," Raine said. "I knew only one Arlanian, my mother, because her people were almost extinct by the time I was born. And I knew few Scinterians because they weren't numerous and almost all were killed in the Great War. But as far as I know, none of them could hide their markings or their eyes." Raine was thoughtful for a moment. "It's something most of the time requires little effort. When I want to hide my eyes, I concentrate on being Scinterian, and when I want to hide my markings, I think about being Arlanian."

The conversation was growing a little somber, so Astrid sought to lighten it. "Except when you're looking at Talan."

This brought the smile back to Raine's face. "The purple of my eyes shows with deep emotion, so I can't hide them at all from her."

Servers brought out trays filled with soft and hard cheeses, fruit, crusty bread, and pastries. Consistent with the communal nature of the Ha'kan, the women serving them were not "servants," rather this was simply their job and the Queen graciously thanked them for their efforts. Astrid, Gimle, and the Queen ate sparingly, but Raine's appetite was exceeded only by Senta's.

"Thank the gods you're here, Senta," Raine said, "or I would look like one of the pigs from the forest."

"From what I understand," Senta replied, "you had more of a work-out this morning than I did."

This was particularly funny as Senta had spent the morning on the training fields in strenuous physical exercise, and it brought smiles all around, including one from Raine.

"You are correct," Raine said, helping herself to seconds.

The women finished their very enjoyable lunch, then rested just a moment in the warm sun as dishes were cleared from the table. A figure on the adjacent terrace caught their eyes. It was Skye, leaning on the railing of the terrace that surrounded the chambers of the Ha'kan heir and her staff. The chambers of the Princess mirrored those of the Queen, and the terraces were connected by a walkway. The attitude of the figure was one of preoccupation, the posture one of dejection.

"Has she been like that all week?" Raine asked.

"Yes," Astrid responded. "Lifa has said that Skye's not really herself right now."

Lifa was Astrid's successor, the future High Priestess, and it was her duty to monitor and report on the well-being of the future royal staff.

Senta set her linen napkin on the table and started to rise. "I'll speak with her."

Raine put her hand on her arm.

"I know Skye's a member of your staff," she said. "But perhaps I could speak to her?"

"I would welcome that," Senta said, and sat back down.

Raine excused herself and crossed the walkway to the adjacent terrace. Skye was indeed lost in thought. She did not notice Raine until she was nearly on top of her, and the Tavinter noticed everything.

"Hello, Raine," Skye said. She might have been a bit morose, but her smile was still warm for her idol.

"And what's this?" Raine said. "You're normally the sun in the summer sky, and today you're the moon on a winter night."

Her friends had tried to elicit conversation from her all week, and Skye had wanted to talk, but could not get the words out. Now, with prompting from the one she adored above all others, the lump in her throat loosened.

"I feel terrible that I've put everyone in danger. And you keep having to save me."

"Okay," Raine said, "the first time I didn't save just you, I saved Dallan, Rika, and some other students as well. And that was purely by accident because I was out hunting Hyr'rok'kin." She and Weynild had come to the aid of the girls when they were still at the Academy, slaughtering well over a hundred of the monstrosities, including a Marrow Shard. "That was great fun," she said, recalling the event fondly.

Skye had to smile a little at the reminder. It had been terrifying, but it was the first time she had met Raine and the dragon.

"And the second time, I didn't really 'save' you, I was just helping Isleif because you were sick. He was really the one who saved you."

Skye did not know how true that was because Raine had created a filament of a connection with Skye to keep her from passing into the Underworld while Isleif removed the poison from her body and soul. And the mention of the wizard's name clouded her expression once more.

"And the third time," Raine said, trying to remember the progression of events, "I 'saved' you from danger I put you in, because you were helping me steal that enchanted stone."

That was true, Skye thought. She had been helping Raine when the sorceress Ingrid had briefly captured her.

"And this last time," Raine's voice drifted off. This last time she had battled an army of Reaper Shards, the wraithlike demons that lived half in the mortal world, half in the Underworld, possibly the most dangerous of all the Hyr'rok'kin. "Okay, this last time, I did save you, but I also saved Senta, Gimle, Dallan, and Rika."

"Yes, but they were defending me! Those things came for me!"

That was true, also, Raine thought. "So, you've been told about Isleif."

"Yes, Talan told me last week."

It was a shock for Skye to learn that the powerful wizard she had revered her entire life was her great-grandfather. Isleif had hoped to shield her from the fate of her mother, who was poisoned by the evil of the Reaper Shards when they discovered her enormous magical power. Everyone believed Skye harbored the same power, although Skye could hardly believe that because her abilities as a mage were middling at best.

"I half think the Reaper Shards came on rumor alone," Skye muttered, disparaging those abilities.

"It doesn't work that way," Raine chided her.

"But that's just it. I'm mediocre as a mage and supposed to possess this great power. And this power that I can't even use has put everyone in danger. The sorceress comes because of me. The Reaper Shards come because of me...."

"And Hel came because of me," Raine said abruptly, cutting her off. "It's my fault that the Goddess of the Underworld now threatens all of Arianthem simply because I'm Arlanian."

"What?" Skye exclaimed, "That's not true! It's not your fault..." She trailed off as the implications of her own words sunk in.

"Oh."

"Skye, none of us can change what we are. I learned that a long time ago, when I wanted to bury the part of me that's Arlanian, thinking it was weak. But I wouldn't be who I am without it." Raine was thoughtful. "Destiny can be a great burden, but I've always believed that destiny is what you make it." She placed her hand on the younger woman's shoulder. "And believe it or not, there will come a day when you will save me."

"Really?" Skye said in disbelief. That did not seem possible, any part of it. It did not seem she was capable of saving Raine, or that Raine would ever need saving. But Raine was insistent.

"Yes. It's been foreseen. Which is why you must concentrate and practice to develop the magic that's in you."

Skye frowned again. She much preferred being on the training field with Dallan and Rika, using her sword and bow.

"Such a face!" Raine said, laughing at her expression. "There are a few fringe benefits to this training, you know."

"What benefits?" Skye asked skeptically.

"Do you see that woman down there?"

Skye followed her gesture. No, she had not seen her, but she hardly knew how that could be.

The woman had long, raven-black hair and sauntered up the steps of the palace. She most definitely was not Ha'kan, although long dark eyelashes flicked to acknowledge the admiring looks from the guards. She wore robes that clung to her curves and a neckline that plunged to her naval, revealing a tantalizing glimpse of full breast with every step. Heat seemed to rise off her, leaving a shimmering trail in her wake, equal parts magic and raw sexuality. The smoldering gaze flicked upward, and the woman laughingly blew a kiss to Raine.

"By the gods," Skye murmured, "who's that?"

"That," Raine said with emphasis, "is your new mentor."

It took a moment for the words to sink in. "What?" Skye exclaimed.

"That's Idonea, Talan's daughter. She's the one who's going to help you develop your skills."

"By the gods," Skye said again.

"Yes, you two will have to spend quite a bit of time together. I hope that's acceptable."

Skye's eyes fairly glowed with excitement, her demeanor having changed completely.

"Yes," she agreed, "I do have a lot of work to do."

Raine could hardly keep up with Skye as she sprinted down the circular stairway, and both arrived at the palace entrance as Idonea stepped through the wrought-iron gate. Skye had an attack of shyness at the last second, however, and Raine strode past her, taking the voluptuous mage in her arms in a light but warm hug. Idonea returned the affection, giving Raine a fond peck of a kiss on her cheek.

"Idonea," Raine said, "thank you for coming. And thank you for your warning."

It had been Idonea who dreamed Skye was in danger and given Raine enough warning to save her from the Reaper Shards.

"I see she's still in one piece," Idonea said, her laughing dark eyes flicking up and down Skye, "so the warning was in time."

"It was perfectly timed."

Skye did not like the fact they were speaking about her like she was not there, as if she were a child. She stepped forward and bowed in a manner worthy of the ruler of the Tavinter. "I am Skye," she said ceremoniously, "welcome to the Ha'kan palace."

"Oh, you are precious," Idonea said, and Skye blushed to the roots of her hair. Any attempt at dignity wilted under the scorching amusement of the raven-haired mage.

Queen Halla and her staff had observed the change in Skye's demeanor and witnessed her enthusiastic departure from the terrace. Curiosity had brought them, too, to the palace entrance. Raine remembered her etiquette as the four approached.

"Your Majesty," she said formally, "this is Idonea, Talan's daughter and Isleif's successor."

Queen Halla took Idonea's hand and pressed it between her own. "Thank you so much for coming," she said warmly.

Idonea examined the lovely, graceful woman. The beauty of the Ha'kan was not exaggerated. All four women, although distinctly different, were gorgeous. The Queen was dark-haired, curvaceous, elegant and stunning. The woman to her left had long, light hair, a slender, willowy figure, and fine features that were complimented by the spectacles she wore. Idonea thought this might be the First Scholar. The very large woman to her left, handsome and imposing, was undoubtedly the First General, her brown eyes sparkling with good humor. And the woman to the Queen's right could be none other than the High Priestess, her exquisite beauty and sensuality as regal as her Queen's.

"I have no idea how you stay faithful to my mother," Idonea said, addressing Raine.

Raine cleared her throat. Idonea never was one for ceremony. But the Ha'kan seemed only entertained by the irreverence, fascinated by the mystical creature in front of them.

"I imagine your journey was long. There are numerous rooms within the palace," Queen Halla said, "and you may choose any you wish. Skye?"

Skye stepped forward. "Yes, your Majesty?"

Astrid hid a smile at Skye's excessive formality, as did Raine.

"Why don't you show Idonea the guest room that's available in Dallan's forum? It's probably the most comfortable and I don't think Dallan would mind."

Skye's eyes glowed at the prospect. Dallan most definitely would not mind. She bowed to Idonea. "If you would follow me."

Idonea ran her fingers through Skye's hair fondly, and Skye once again blushed crimson. The women watched the two leave, and Senta noted that Skye's step was far lighter than she had seen it in days.

"Well, that can only be good for the girl," Senta commented.

"She's got a bit of her mother in her, doesn't she?" Gimle murmured, speaking of Idonea.

"She grows more like her every day," Raine replied, shaking her head. "The Divine help us all."

Skye led Idonea to Dallan's forum, the circular living chambers a duplicate of the Queen's. Unlike most of Arianthem, it was traditional for the Ha'kan to undergo a very benign succession. At some point, Queen Halla would simply relinquish her throne to her daughter, and she and her entire staff would become cherished advisors. Although Halla's mother had passed some years earlier, the former First Scholar still lived within the palace. The former High Priestess maintained a suite there but chose to spend most of her time in the town of her birth where she was fairly worshipped.

To ease that transition, the younger generation of Ha'kan held positions that paralleled their predecessors. Skye explained the living arrangements as they entered the forum.

"That's Dallan's room," she said, pointing across the community area, "and next to it is Lifa's room, the future High Priestess."

Idonea examined the stately but comfortable forum. It had a large, stone fire pit in the center surrounded by couches. "Although most of the time, Lifa stays at the Ministry Building," Skye continued. "And really, everyone spends most of their time there, and many nights."

"And why is that?" Idonea asked innocently.

Skye colored a bit. "Well, there are three castes in Ha'kan society, Warriors, Scholars, and Priestesses. And the Ministry houses the Priestesses."

"And?"

Skye cleared her throat. "Well, you know. The Priestesses provide pleasure for all who want or need it."

"Sexual pleasure?" Idonea said, sounding shocked, and Skye realized she was teasing her.

"Yes," Skye said primly, "sexual pleasure."

Idonea was pleased to see the girl begin to stand up to her.

"Kara is the future First Scholar," Skye said, resuming her role as tour guide, "and her room is there. And Rika is Senta's successor, and her chambers are there. And then this is my room. It's the one difference between the Queen's forum and Dallan's, since my position is new for the Ha'kan."

"Well, shouldn't you actually be in the Queen's forum? Since you're the head of the Tavinter Rangers?"

"By the gods, no!" Skye exclaimed, eliciting a low, throaty chuckle from Idonea that reminded Skye very much of Talan. Technically that was true, but Skye had attended the Academy with Dallan and her cohort, and so remained with them. She could barely handle the distracting sexuality of the young Ha'kan, and being in the presence of the Royal Staff was overwhelming. Although she did occasionally share the bed of the First General, Skye usually scurried through the Queen's forum, praying that she would not run into the sultry elegance of the High Priestess or Queen. Even working with Gimle was a trial in concentration.

"And this will be your room," Skye said, pushing through the door. It was laid out as the others, with a front room lavishly furnished and designed for entertaining guests, then a back bedroom with closets, bookshelves, and an enormous bed also designed for entertaining guests. Several robes had been laid out on the blanket, and a basket of fruit and various sundries, soap, lotion and the like, on the nightstand. Skye nodded toward a table and chairs that could serve multiple purposes.

"You're welcome to eat here if you wish, but the Ha'kan always eat together. In fact," Skye corrected herself, "they do everything together. And it's my experience that they'll welcome you to every part of it."

"Every part of it?" Idonea said with a slight lift of her eyebrow, and for once Skye did not blush at the innuendo. She examined the voluptuous mage in front of her. "Oh yes," she said, "without a doubt."

The Ha'kan, although resembling human females, were an entirely separate race. Their reproduction was independent of sexual activity and attributed to the mother alone via parthenogenesis. This quirk of reproduction greatly shaped and influenced their society and culture. The Ha'kan rarely experimented sexually outside their own race simply because it was so very dissatisfying. And generally speaking, they were not attracted to non-Ha'kan. Skye had proven an unusual exception and was fully embraced by the insular people. She thought the Ha'kan would likely make an exception for Idonea as well.

"Well, now there's something to look forward to," Idonea mused, "although I've likely complicated things, which I imagine will become apparent when the imperials arrive."

The comment was curious, but Skye would not pry.

"Is there anything else you need?" Skye asked. "I believe Talan is out patrolling but should return any time. I'm not scheduled for lessons with

Gimle until tomorrow, and it's already late in the afternoon. Perhaps you'd like to rest before evening meal?"

Idonea tousled Skye's hair again, eliciting the color Skye thought she had successfully banished from her cheeks.

"That would be fine, my little Tavinter."

Skye sat in the common area about the fire pit, studying her books. Not only was she in charge of the Tavinter Rangers, required to train as a member of the Warrior caste, and supposed to study magic with Gimle, she was still trying to make up her studies from the Academy. For a number of reasons, she had spent only a year at the four-year institution, and she had been at a disadvantage there because the Tavinter were raised and educated very differently than the Ha'kan. Although the Ha'kan had learned to appreciate the talents and differences of the Tavinter, Skye still wanted to complete her formal education. Kara, her normal tutor in this matter, flowed into the room in her typical dreamy manner. Skye and the books caught her eye and she came up behind her, placing her hands on her shoulders and leaning over to see what she was studying.

"Oh," Kara said with pleasure, "mathematics. One of my favorites. Do you need help?"

"You know I always do," Skye said.

"And what's this?" Kara said, picking up the book next to Skye on the couch. "Disa's Treatise on Anatomy," she said, reading the title aloud. "Now you know this is my favorite subject of all."

Kara's voice acquired an undertone that Skye knew well, one that inspired equal parts nervousness and anticipation in her. Outwardly, Kara was reserved, controlled, focused on her research and experiments. Beneath that staid exterior, however, she was wickedly eccentric, possessing all the heat and passion of the Ha'kan. That passion was magnified by that focus and control and expressed through a near-infinite imagination and unrepressed sense of humor. Skye was one of her very favorite test subjects.

Kara leaned down, placing her arms about Skye's neck. "So, perhaps you need some tutoring this evening?"

Skye turned so that her cheek was pressed against Kara's lips. Kara was a bit frightening, but Skye so loved her. "That would be wonderful," she replied, "the Scholar's loft or your chambers here?"

Due to her position, Kara maintained a loft in the wing that housed the Scholars as she often worked late and slept odd hours.

"I'm thinking here, around 7th bell."

Skye was relieved. In the personal chambers, Kara would not have access to the endless array of contraptions strewn about her lab. Skye's relief was short-lived.

"I brought a few experiments back, some things I thought we could try."

"Hmm," was all Skye said, and Kara kissed her, laughing as she stood upright. Rika strode in at that moment.

"Someone's in a good mood," she said. She took one look at Skye's face and discerned the cause. "Ah, some scholarly research this evening."

Rika was much like Senta, large, handsome, and good-humored. She was not quite as reserved as the imposing First General and could be ribald and even rowdy. But she took her responsibilities seriously, both those current and future. Currently she and Dallan were in charge of an entire regiment, Rika assuming command when Dallan was pulled away to fulfill her royal duties. Skye did not know if Rika consciously emulated Senta, but her carriage and demeanor mimicked that of the general. They could be standing next to one another in exactly the same stance, arms crossed about their chest, the same look on their face. It was evident Rika greatly admired the First General.

"And what are you studying?" Rika asked.

Kara held up the book. "We're doing some review on anatomy."

"I believe I'm in need of review," Rika said, "what perfect timing!"

Skye muffled a snort. "You're in a constant state of anatomy review. So short a memory from last night? Or perhaps it was this afternoon?"

Rika winked.

A gleam came into Kara's eye and Skye had a sense of foreboding. "The future First General is always welcome as both observer and participant."

"What?" Skye exclaimed.

"Well, if you don't want me in your bed," Rika said in mock hurt.

Skye snorted again. That was as unlikely a scenario possible, and she did not even rise to the bait.

Rika grinned. "I'll let you be sky, Skye."

Both Skye and Kara brightened at that prospect. "Really?" Skye said. That would be great fun. For the Ha'kan, earth and sky were playful references to how dominant a woman was in bed. Skye had spent most of her first experiences as "earth" until she realized that for the Ha'kan, all things sexual were open to negotiation, and in practical terms, all she had to do was ask.

A smaller auburn-haired woman flowed into the room behind Rika and the world instantly seemed both warmer and brighter. Lifa was not small, for none of the Ha'kan were. She was just slightly shorter and far shapelier, perfectly rounded with silken robes that draped and clung in a manner that emphasized the womanly perfection of her form. She, too, emulated her mentor, and the sultry elegance of the High Priestess was more evident every day. She also possessed the intuition of her mentor, especially when it involved sexual matters, and she interpreted the expressions in the room without effort.

"Discussing evening arrangements?" Lifa said, laughter in her warm brown eyes. She was happy to see Kara so engaged as Kara often disappeared for days at a time, lost in her research. It was Lifa's responsibility to see to the sexual health and bonding of the Ha'kan as whole, but also very specifically that of Dallan's staff. Kara could become distant, elusive, a challenge, but both Skye and Rika were gifted at bringing Kara back into the fold.

"Yes," Rika said, "would you like to join us?"

Both Skye and Kara looked at Lifa expectantly, and she was genuinely disappointed she had to decline.

"I would love to, but I have some official duties to perform this evening."

Rika assessed the response, eyes narrowed. Lifa approached all of her obligations with quiet joy, but she seemed a bit too joyful at tonight's duties. Rika nudged Kara in the ribs. "She's going to spend the night in Astrid's bed."

Lifa smiled demurely, but the twitch at the corner of that lovely mouth gave her away. "You know I must learn all I can from my mentor."

Rika sprawled on the couch across from Skye. "By the gods, I should have been a Priestess."

Both Skye and Kara burst into laughter at this pronouncement, just as Dallan walked in.

"What did I miss?" Dallan asked as Rika looked blackly at the laughing pair.

"Can you imagine Rika as a Priestess?" Skye said.

Dallan's own dark eyes twinkled with mirth. As the rest of her staff mirrored their mentors, she mirrored the beauty of her mother. She was a bit more lithe and lanky in build, but that was likely due to the days spent on the training fields. The Princess of the Ha'kan was greatly beloved, recognized for her courage and skill in battle, and she was becoming renowned for her grace and diplomacy. Such diplomacy and tact sought to manifest itself.

"Of course," Dallan said, "I can imagine Rika as anything she wants to be."

Skye and Kara looked at her pointedly, and the future Queen of the Ha'kan dissolved and there was simply Dallan.

"All right, that didn't sound convincing even to me."

Everyone burst into laughter once more.

"Thank you, my friend," Rika said, again feigning hurt. But she could no more disguise her good humor than Dallan her personality, and she joined the laughter.

The door to the guest room was open and movement caught Dallan's eye.

"Who's that?" she murmured.

Skye was deliberately casual, something all but Lifa missed. She was gifted at recognizing and reading body language, a part of her innate abilities as future High Priestess. But then again, Skye was never that difficult to read. The Tavinter was abruptly, studiously examining the book in her lap, a little smile on her lips.

Rika, too, leaned forward, trying to peer into the guest room with little if any subtlety. She got a glimpse of the figure moving around inside.

"I don't know," she said.

"Skye," Lifa said, "who is that?"

"What?" Skye said, still casual. "Oh, that's Idonea." She addressed Dallan. "Your mother didn't think you would mind."

Both Dallan's and Rika's eyes were still glued to the doorway. But this last pronouncement caused Dallan to turn to Skye, confused. "My mother? But who's Idonea?"

"I am Idonea."

All eyes swiveled about as the woman walked into the forum. Idonea had changed into one of the robes provided, really the most revealing of all of them, and it clung as if by magic in all the right places. It seemed something would spill forth, so precariously were those curves clothed, but somehow that most delightful was just barely concealed. That did not stop Rika from watching vigilantly, just in case.

Skye was enjoying the stunned expressions on the Ha'kan faces. "Idonea is my mentor."

"Forget being a Priestess," Rika muttered, "now if only I were a mage."

"You must be the future First General," Idonea said. The Ha'kan had lined up to greet her, and Rika led the charge, remembering her manners.

"I'm Rika," she said, extending her hand, "welcome to the palace."

Idonea took the hand, examining it. "My, they grow them big here."

The comment greatly pleased Rika and she took it as a compliment as intended. Idonea moved on to Lifa.

"And you have to be the future High Priestess."

Lifa extended her hand gracefully, all smiles for the raven-haired beauty in front of her. "Yes," she said warmly, "I'm Lifa. Welcome."

Idonea returned the smile gently, a rarity of a response. Lifa instinctively understood the honor bestowed upon her. This was a creature of fire and ice, whose demeanor rarely tempered to anything between, especially genuine warmth. Idonea moved on to Kara.

"And you must be the future First Scholar."

The woman already fascinated Kara, not only because she was a powerful mage, but because she had a wildness about her that was intriguing. And Idonea determined that she liked the Ha'kan scholars. They were outwardly calm, cool, and reserved, but she could tell they had fire in their veins, fire that most likely came out in a reckless, slightly unbalanced manner she could relate to.

"I'm Kara. Although I have no talent with magic, I assist both Gimle and Skye with research, so I'm at your disposal."

"Well, that will be fun now, won't it?"

Rika snorted as Idonea moved on to the last member of the group. She examined the young woman for some time.

"And you must be the Princess."

"Yes, I am Dal-lan."

Lifa turned to look down the row at Dallan. Dallan was charming, charismatic, smooth, composed, and articulate, master of all social situations. But her voice had just cracked like that of a 14-year-old boy. Kara cleared her throat and Skye made a pained noise as she tried to suppress her laughter. Rika made no such attempt at self-control and fairly guffawed.

Dallan clenched her jaw, cleared her throat, and collected herself. "Yes, I'm Dallan. Welcome to the palace."

Idonea took a moment longer to assess the Ha'kan princess, enjoying the discomfort she was causing. Dallan tried to be patient beneath the assessment. She was usually supremely confident, unruffled in all matters, especially those sexual in nature. But for whatever reason, the seductive dragon Talan had always flustered her. And now it seemed her daughter would have the same effect.

"Please let me know if there's anything I can provide you during your stay. The Ha'kan are at your service."

"Thank you, the hospitality of the Ha'kan is legendary." Idonea let her fish off the hook and turned to Skye. "I'm going to wander about the grounds, and then I'm dining with Raine. But I'll take you up on your offer of dinner soon."

"And we have lessons tomorrow afternoon," Skye reminded her.

Idonea ruffled her hair and for once Skye did not blush. "How could I forget?"

All eyes followed the mage from the room, and then a short silence ensued.

"I-am-Dal-lan," Rika said in a very stilted voice, her voice cracking on the last word.

The group again erupted into mirth and Lifa, although as entertained as the rest, tried to temper her merriment. She put her hand soothingly on Dallan's cheek.

"You do have a problem with those dragons, don't you?"

Dallan's expression was dark, but the darkness was giving way to Lifa's gentle touch and her friends' merriment. Even though it was at her expense, she had to admit, it was funny. Having Talan in the castle all week had been nerve-wracking and she sought to avoid the dragon queen who somehow always made her feel like she was a bumbling adolescent. It seemed her daughter, although half-human and not actually a dragon, had inherited a great deal from her mother.

"Kara's giving Skye some anatomy lessons tonight, and I'm sitting in as review. We have room for a fourth," Rika suggested.

Multiple partners were neither the norm nor unusual for the Ha'kan, and at times the situation seemed more appropriate than others. It seemed very fitting at the moment.

"That sounds like an excellent idea," Dallan said.

"So, I understand you've already embarrassed Dallan," Raine said, "good for you."

Idonea was seated in Raine's chamber at the multi-purpose table. A bevy of servers had swarmed in, set the table, served the food, then just as quickly disappeared, leaving a wonderful meal and a few lingering glances of appreciation behind.

"She's smitten with your mother, although that crush usually displays itself by her running the other direction. I feel sorry for the Princess. She's had her way with women since birth, and then Weynild shows up and flusters her without end."

"That's the effect my mother usually has on people. Equal parts lust and terror."

"A mantle you're beginning to wear yourself quite well," Raine said, taking a sip of the chilled white wine Idonea favored.

Twenty years ago, a comparison between her and her mother would have infuriated Idonea. Now, she had to acknowledge, it filled her with pride.

"And I understand you stopped to see Isleif on your way here. How's he doing?"

"He's weak," Idonea said, "and he fades. I think he holds on only to protect Skye. I fear once he feels she's safe and prepared, he'll let go."

"That must fill you with mixed emotions regarding your task, then."

"Yes and no," Idonea responded, taking a sip of her wine. "It gives it an air of sadness, but makes it no less necessary."

"You're gaining your mother's sight, as well," Raine said shrewdly.

"A little," Idonea said. "I don't see with any of the clarity of my mother, or of Isleif or Y'arren. But I begin to sense how things are unfolding."

"And is that what motivated your little tryst in the imperial capital?" Raine said, lightening the subject.

This prompted a long drink from Idonea, then a wicked smile that reminded Raine very much of Weynild.

"Not entirely. The Knight Commander was surprisingly entertaining."

Raine grinned. "Everyone was shocked that the imperials de-escalated the situation with the heir to the House of Storr."

"But not you."

"No, I saw the Knight Commander fumble about whenever she got around you. That fling was inevitable."

"So, I'm guessing it was you who suggested the imperials and Alfar meet here as a compromise."

"Not directly," Raine said, "I might have mentioned something to Feyden, who might have relayed something to his sister."

Feyden was one of the Alfar, the high elves that lived on Mount Alfheim. Although the Alfar were a proud people who looked down upon nearly every other race, Feyden was a dear friend to both Idonea and Raine, the latter whom he worshipped. Two decades before, the three had been part of an intrepid band that had traveled through the Empty Land, then through the Veil to shut the Gate of the Underworld and stem the flow of Hyr'rok'kin into the mortal realm. Feyden's twin sister Maeva, his elder by minutes, was about to become Directorate of the Alfar, the closest thing the Alfar had to a supreme leader. Maeva was currently on a diplomatic mission in Arianthem to assess potential alliances and had already signed a treaty with the Dverger. But the dwarves and elves, although physically very different, shared both history and culture. In contrast, Maeva found little in common with the imperials and harbored an intense dislike of the sons and daughters of men.

"Do you really think she took that girl to her bed?"

"I don't know," Raine said. "It doesn't sound like something Maeva would do. Her disdain for humankind is well known."

But it made as much sense as anything else, Raine thought to herself. She and Weynild had been working to foster an alliance between the Alfar and imperials when Maeva had created a diplomatic firestorm by kidnapping the daughter of the largest landowner in all of Arianthem. The Lord and Lady Storr owned the entire swath of land that bordered Alfar territory, so its strategic importance could not be overstated. But the gentle couple were notoriously reclusive, and no one, not even the excellent spies of the Alfar, knew that the Lord and Lady had been dead for several years. No one knew, that is, until the young daughter had responded to an invitation to a soiree at one of Maeva's estates, then promptly disappeared.

"I have no idea," Raine said, shaking her head. "But thank the divine you seduced the Knight Commander."

"I hardly see what that has to do with anything," Idonea said with false modesty. Raine looked over the top of her wine glass wryly.

"Nerthus had no reason to compromise with the Alfar, and every excuse to respond with force. And yet suddenly she's a model of restraint because the proposed compromise involves a trip to the Ha'kan capital, where you just happen to be."

The dark-haired beauty laughed and Raine had a glimpse of the "old" Idonea, the one who cared nothing for the machinations of nations and acted with wanton recklessness simply because she could.

"Attribute whatever nobility you want," Idonea said, "the Knight Commander is a fabulous romp in the hay."

"Well, that's just what every mother wants to hear," Weynild said as she came in from the terrace. Raine was surprised; she almost always heard the tell-tale leathery wings of Weynild's arrival, or at least the sound of her alighting. As graceful as she was, the enormous size of the creature alone ensured the landing would not be quiet. She and Idonea had been very engaged in their conversation.

"Quite a comment, coming from you," Idonea responded.

"You mistake truth for sarcasm," Weynild said, leaning down to kiss her daughter's cheek. "That is indeed what every dragon mother wants to hear."

Raine grinned, for that was probably true. Dragons were known for their insatiable lust, and it was likely they would only admire such a trait in their offspring. As if to emphasize the point, Weynild gave Raine a lengthy, searing kiss in full view of Idonea.

"Are you two going to fuck right in front of me?"

Raine muffled laughter, and Weynild's golden eyes slid around to her daughter.

"Now, it wouldn't be the first time, would it?"

Idonea rolled her eyes. "You're never going to let me forget that, are you?"

Many years ago, on their quest, Idonea had come upon her mother and Raine in a passionate embrace. Instead of revealing herself, Idonea remained hidden, unable to look away. Weynild knew the girl was spying on them, but instead of stopping, unleashed an epic sexual performance. She then looked directly at Idonea to let her know she was aware of her presence. To an outside observer, it would have seemed very strange, but it was very typical, dragon-like discipline.

"Not in my lifetime," Weynild said, a statement with particular weight as the dragon was essentially immortal.

Weynild sat down next to Raine and for a moment, the two had eyes only for one another.

"Would you like me to leave?"

"I beg your pardon, Idonea. I'm being rude," Raine said. "Your mother and I've been apart a lot lately, and I can't say I like it."

This comment caused Weynild to grow serious for a moment. "And how are you feeling?"

"I'm fine," Raine said, but her overly dismissive attitude attracted Idonea's attention.

"What happened?" she asked.

Raine's expression grew grim. "After you warned me, I arrived barely in time. Skye was already under attack from Reaper Shards, maybe a dozen of them."

"By the gods," Idonea murmured. One was terrifying and could destroy an entire town. She had never heard of so many manifesting in a single place.

"There was a magical barrier in place, right out there," Raine said, nodding in the direction of the palace courtyard, "that kept Skye and her protectors separated from help. Fortunately, Gimle and Senta, as well as Dallan and Rika, were inside the barrier and held them off until I could arrive."

"And you were able to pass through the barrier?"

Raine's unique parentage gave her a priceless gift: a total immunity to magic. "Yes, I was a little concerned about the weapons you enchanted for me. And even a little worried about my clothes," Raine said, half to herself.

As serious as the subject was, Weynild had to smile at the thought of her lover coming through the barrier wearing nothing more than her markings.

"The weapons were fantastic," Raine continued. "Your spells cut the Reapers down like wheat before a scythe."

"Isleif thought that a combination of natural magic and light would work."

"He was right."

Raine grew quiet, and Idonea's gaze went to her mother, then back to Raine.

"And then what happened?" Idonea asked.

"The remaining Reapers disappeared. And then the Membrane came."

Raine grew pale at the mention of the atrocity, and Idonea shared her horror. She could picture the demonic apparition. The Membrane was cursed beyond all other miscreations, an oily, yellowish amalgam of limbs and sexual parts, created from the souls that Hel had doomed to eternal damnation. The monstrosity was in perpetual, painful orgasm, forced to endlessly pleasure itself, the lips, tongues, breasts, fingers, and sexual organs engaged in every type of deviant act imaginable.

"I feared, many years ago, when you saved me and Gunnar from that creature, that it would gain an affinity towards you," Idonea said quietly.

When they were in the midst of the Veil, the filmy realm that separated the mortal world from the Underworld, the Membrane had appeared and at first touched Gunnar, an imperial knight who was heading their expedition. It was then attracted to Idonea and the Black Magic in her it desired to feed upon above all else. Raine distracted the creature from Idonea by revealing her eyes and Arlanian heritage. The Membrane had set upon her in a delighted frenzy of lust, and she was able to freeze it with a breath of air, a fortuitous side-effect of the collision between absolute purity and absolute evil. It did not destroy the Membrane, for the Membrane could not be destroyed. It could only be rendered impotent for a short time.

"Gunnar never recovered from the Membrane's touch," Raine said, a faraway look in her eye. "It poisoned him with fear and indecision."

"And it touched you again?" Idonea asked.

"Yes," Raine said, her mind in a very dark place, "For—"

Her voice trailed off and Weynild took her hand and squeezed it. Raine shook her head to clear it.

"For a very long time."

Idonea understood what Raine was not saying. If the Membrane lingered on her at all, then it had practically raped her.

"And that wasn't the worst of it," Weynild added.

Idonea knew there was only one thing worse than the Membrane.

"Hel appeared again."

"Yes," Weynild said. "She, too, has acquired an affinity for my little Arlanian."

There was far more to it than that, Idonea thought. She did not know all the details, but there was history between Hel and her mother that did not bode well for Raine.

Now it was Raine that squeezed Weynild's hand. "But my love arrived just in time to save me."

It seemed the weight of the conversation was too much for Raine and she suddenly felt and appeared greatly fatigued. Weynild brushed her cheek with her hand.

"I think you should go lie down."

"I should leave," Idonea said, and made as if to stand.

"I would ask you to stay a moment longer," Weynild said. "I'll put her to bed and return."

Weynild was true to her word, escorting Raine to bed but returning a minute later. She sat down across from her daughter once more. It was Idonea who broke the silence.

"So, how did you save Raine?"

"I was scouting the Empty Land, and when I sensed what was occurring, I moved through Nifelheim," Weynild said.

"That was dangerous," Idonea commented.

That was an understatement. Nifelheim was part of Hel's realm, another netherworld between life and death. It was inhabited by creatures more dangerous than Reaper Shards, and even Talan, one of the twelve Ancients, could end up in fierce battle there.

"It wasn't my intent to use the fade bracelet that way, nor this soon," Weynild said. She and Raine had completed the magical artifact by replacing its missing stones. The bracelet could render the wearer invisible by allowing them to skirt the periphery of Nifelheim. However,Weynild had not stayed on the periphery, but rather had used the bracelet to cut through the heart of the demonic world.

"It was necessary."

"What does Hel want from Raine?"

Weynild's tone was cynical. "What do you think she wants?"

"Okay, perhaps a better question is why?"

The obvious answer to Hel's lust was because Raine was Arlanian, that the last of the irresistible people was too choice a target. But Weynild knew that wasn't what Idonea was getting at and she was silent for a moment.

"You have my blood, which means you have all of my lust. I've been hard on you at times, perhaps even hypocritical in my efforts to get you to exercise good judgment in fulfilling your needs."

Idonea said nothing, for that certainly was true.

"That's only because I want you to have better judgment than I, to avoid the mistakes that I've made."

This was significant. There were few repercussions for something as powerful as a dragon, and little in the terms of conscience that would affect them. Her mother rarely admitted mistakes because she did not feel she had made many.

"Although Raine is certainly desirable enough to attract Hel's eye on her own, I believe some of Hel's fervor is due to my past indiscretions."

It was some time before Weynild's words could fully take hold, and when they did, Idonea was stunned.

"You?" she said in disbelief. "And Hel?"

"Yes. I was quite," she paused, searching for an appropriate description "vigorous as a young dragon."

"You fucked a goddess?"

"Yes dear," Weynild said drily, "I fucked a goddess."

Idonea's laughter spilled forth. "Oh mother, that's something even for you." She leaned forward. "And how did it end?"

"As most dealings with the gods, it ended badly."

"No!" Idonea exclaimed, leaning back, her eyes glowing with pleasure, "You dumped her."

"This is exactly how I knew you would respond to this conversation," Weynild said with disapproval. But the disapproval was difficult to generate and even harder to maintain, for Idonea was responding exactly as she would were their positions reversed.

"Oh mother, come now. I know you've been a philanderer your whole life. But a god? I can't let this one go."

"Yes, yes. Enjoy it. It was an enormously bad decision. Pleasurable? Yes. Wise? No. And I've spent my whole life wondering how she would take her revenge, even fearing she would take it out on you."

This sobered Idonea because her thoughts returned to Raine.

"So Raine is in immense danger."

"Yes."

"Does she know all this?"

"Oh yes," Weynild said, "there's nothing I keep from my love."

"So, all of this, the Hyr'rok'kin invasions, is that—?"

"My fault?" Weynild finished for her. "At times I blame myself, but in truth, that began before anything happened between Hel and me. I think that's a battle between the gods themselves, a constant skirmish over the borders of the mortal realm, the Underworld, and perhaps even Ásgarðr itself."

"But it probably didn't help."

"No," Weynild said, her tone even drier than before. "I'm sure it didn't help."

Idonea relented, growing contemplative. "Interesting how the past influences the present. Skye is pursued by that sorceress for Isleif's indiscretions."

"And Raine is pursued for mine. Although I do believe both are desirable enough to generate such negative attention on their own. But it does seem Arianthem would be a far more peaceful place if all the magical creatures could just 'keep it in their pants,' so to speak."

It was more of an observation than a criticism from Weynild, for she could not produce self-reproach for something that was so integral to her nature. The observation equally applied to Idonea, and it seemed she could not generate much contrition, either.

"Well how boring would that be?" she said.

CHAPTER 2

Raine propped her elbows on the hay bale, watching the Ha'kan on the training fields. It had been lost in all the serious conversation the night before, but Weynild had told her sleepily this morning that the Alfar were still a week away, and the imperials were behind them. So, she had another week to relax in the Ha'kan capital, and her lover took full advantage of this by rolling over and going back to sleep.

But Raine could not sleep and rose from bed. And instead of the luxurious robes she had been wearing lately, she pulled on her armor. It brought a serenity to her that few things did. The leather armor had a unique bluish cast to it and fit her perfectly, shaped to her form and moving as if it were part of her. Truly, it fit her almost as well as Weynild's scaled armor. The elaborately carved weapon rack by the door also drew her. She left her bow, longsword, and assortment of daggers there, but she took the two short swords and inserted them into the sheaths strapped crossways on her back. It felt good and she stretched her limbs, then headed out the terrace and down the stairs to the courtyard.

And now she leaned against the hay in bright morning light. The sky was turning a pale blue, the pastel ribbons of dawn fading into the rising sun. A light frost was on the grass and a light mist still lingered. The Ha'kan were just assembling. She could see Senta on one side and Rika on the other, both shouting orders. Dallan and Skye were preparing to warm up with a sword drill. Soon everyone was engaged in some sort of strenuous practice, for Ha'kan warriors loved to train.

And so did Raine. She felt the itch in her palm to be holding a sword. Although her skills were so ingrained, she could probably go years without missing a beat or getting rusty, even a few days of inactivity grated on her. And the week she had just spent in bed taxed her sorely.

The First General seemed to be reading her mind, or perhaps just her longing expression, and approached the hay barrier. "Would you like to train with the Royal Guard?" Senta asked.

Raine flashed her a brilliant smile. "I would be honored," she said, and vaulted the barrier with ease. Senta watched the effortless maneuver and grinned herself. The Royal Guard, the elite of the Ha'kan forces, were in for a treat today. The two jogged over to a group of women, all very large and dressed in full armor. The Royal Guard almost always trained in full gear, and Raine looked small next to them. Although very muscular, she was lithe and not large-framed.

The Royal Guard knew who approached them. They had heard the Scinterian was in the capital and staying in the palace, and some had even seen her when on duty, admiring her striking looks. They shifted with excitement, even a little nervousness at the possibility of seeing her in action. But Ha'kan warriors liked to fight, and the Royal Guard more so than any.

"I'd like to volunteer first," said one brave soul, stepping forward.

"I don't know, Raine," Senta said, nudging her in the ribs. "Hildr is kind of big."

Raine glanced up at the First General. "Not as big as you," Raine murmured, "and not as big as a Marrow Shard."

Senta laughed and waved for the contest to begin. Raine's opponent attempted to catch her off-guard and lunged forward before Raine had even drawn her swords. But the swords came out in a flashing, twirling motion, trapping the longer sword between the hilts. This maneuver allowed Raine to place her boot on Hildr's shield and push her solidly backward. Raine was delighted with the attempt at trickery, for this was nothing more than play to her.

"I'm going to need some help with this," Hildr said good-naturedly, and another woman at her side joined in the battle.

"Look over there," Skye said to Dallan. "Raine is training with the Royal Guard."

Dallan stopped what she was doing. Raine seemed engaged with three or four opponents. "We have to go watch."

Rika saw Dallan and Skye dart across the training field, then saw their destination. She addressed Rona, her second. "I'm going to see what's going on over there."

There was a look of exhilaration on Raine's face as the Royal Guard rotated in and she battled multiple opponents. They would rotate out as they grew fatigued, but Raine showed no signs of tiring. Other than a light sheen of sweat on her brow, she did not show any signs of exertion. Were it any other opponent, Senta would have been displeased at the results from the battle-hardened Royal Guard. But this was a creature who was born to fight, and there was not another warrior like her in all Arianthem.

"Can I rotate in?" Dallan asked Senta.

"Of course, your Highness," Senta said. "You're next."

Raine turned to her next opponent and grinned when she saw it was Dallan. Dallan was one of the best in swordplay of all the Ha'kan. As Raine had done from the start, she adjusted her style to that of her challenger. Dallan was fast and highly technical and their swords were a blur as they lunged, parried, feinted, countered, all the while moving about with beautiful footwork.

Queen Halla watched the contest from the terrace above. Were it any other opponent she might have been fearful for her lovely daughter, so pitched and fierce was that battle, but instead she was only proud. She became aware of a figure next to her and turned to Weynild, whose tall, lean figure was draped beautifully in a green satin robe. Halla gazed at her appreciatively, her eyes lingering on the swell of breast above the robe, the brief glance a compliment but not so bold as to suggest anything more.

"I see my love is out playing."

"Yes," Halla said, "she seems intent on engaging the entire Ha'kan army."

"Your daughter's quite skilled," Weynild commented, "I can tell by the joy on Raine's face."

"Skye!" exclaimed Dallan, laughing as she fell back, "Get in here and help me!"

It took no coercion at all for Skye to jump into the make-shift arena the crowd of onlookers had created. She held a sword in one hand and a dagger in the other, fighting in the Tavinter style that rarely utilized shields. They were not a large people, so they used avoidance and misdirection far more than brute force.

And now Raine was truly challenged, for she had to defend against two distinctly different styles of fighting. In truth, part of her challenge was to avoid hurting her opponents because it was much easier just to kill someone rather than prolong the fight. But Skye and Dallan were a deadly combination and the Royal Guard, as well as a few Tavinter Scouts, were cheering them on raucously.

"Rika!" Skye said, out of breath from both laughter and exertion, "Get in here!"

And Rika did not hesitate to join the fray. Senta debated stopping the contest because it was becoming more of a free-for-all brawl than a training exercise. But, she mused, the troops could wind up in such circumstances, and besides, it was humorous to watch.

Rika gave up all pretense of fighting fairly and the minute Skye dived in with a quick jab that distracted Raine, she grabbed Raine in a bear hug from behind and lifted her from her feet, reasoning that removing her leverage might even the fight.

It did no such thing. Without hesitation, Raine dropped both swords, flung her leg rearward and hooked her ankle behind Rika's knee, then yanked it forward. This caused Rika to buckle and Raine to regain her feet just enough to lean forward, pulling Rika even more off balance. Then in an astonishing display of strength, she lifted Rika off the ground, whose arms were still around Raine, no longer restraining her but now hanging on for dear life.

Dallan dropped her sword and rushed in to aid her hapless friend, but that was a mistake because Raine pivoted and swung Rika's legs around so they struck Dallan squarely in the midsection, knocking the wind from her. Raine worked her arm upward beneath Rika's, giving just enough control to set Rika down upon her feet once more, then promptly throw her over her shoulder. Rika nearly landed on Dallan and would have had Dallan not quickly rolled out of the way.

Raine sensed the movement as Skye sought to tackle her from behind, and in a move worthy of a Tavinter, stepped out of the way, swept Skye's feet from beneath her, and both went tumbling down on top of Rika and Dallan. All four were a stumbling, bumbling mess of tangled limbs and laughter. Senta knew she should end the brawl, but it looked like so much fun she thought about joining in herself. She had an unknown supporter, however, probably the only one who could stop the fight instantly.

Raine felt herself plucked from the ground and lifted as if she weighed nothing. Weynild, now clothed in her dragonscale armor, dangled her from the back of her collar as if she were an ill-behaved pup. Raine's feet were a good foot off the ground as Weynild suspended her in front of her, gazing at her mockingly.

"Are you picking on the Ha'kan?"

There was a lovely blush to Raine's cheeks, part exertion, part embarrassment at her predicament, but mostly pleasure at the display of strength from her lover.

"So, are you going to challenge me now?"

"We know how that will end," Weynild said, her tone still mocking but now with a sensual undertone.

Raine turned to Skye, mouthing words that could barely be heard but easily discerned.

"I will be earth," she said, and Skye's musical laughter burst forth because it was a private joke between the two of them. When Skye had been ill and feverish, she had asked Raine a very personal question regarding whether she was "earth or sky." Raine had breezily answered that she was earth most of the time, greatly surprising Skye that the deadliest warrior in all of Arianthem was, well, usually on the bottom in bed.

Weynild set Raine on her feet, and Raine leaned forward and stole a quick kiss, causing a flash of violet to appear in her own eyes. The act amused the dragon because it was perhaps more mischievous and dangerous than anything that preceded it. And the Ha'kan, who had been greatly entertained by the comical melee, now were greatly enamored by the sight of the dragon and her lover. And Rika, who understood monogamy not at all, once again mused that the two were a perfectly matched pair.

"I'll remove this ruffian from your ranks," Weynild said to Senta. "She seems to be disruptive."

"A little disruption is a good thing," Senta said. She then nodded to Raine. "And you're welcome to train with us anytime."

"Thank you," Raine said, her white teeth brilliant in her smile. "It was great fun."

All watched as the two walked arm-in-arm from the field.

"Do you think we gave her much of a work-out at all?" Hildr asked Senta.

"It's hard to say," Senta said diplomatically.

"I don't think so," Skye interjected with no diplomacy at all. "Her markings didn't even show."

So Raine was indeed earth for the next few hours, and then lay lazily in her lover's arms in the early afternoon.

"I think Haldis is becoming my third favorite place in Arianthem," Raine said.

"Third? What's your second?"

Weynild did not ask about the first because she knew it was the mountain keep where Raine had first stumbled upon her decades before. That was a simple, rustic place, little more than an enormous cave, but it was utterly private and all else ceased to exist when they were there together.

"The cottage in the Wilds, of course."

"Ah, of course." This was much like her Arlanian, for Raine owned the most luxurious residence in the imperial capital, rivaled only by the imperial palace itself. Yet that had not ranked top three, and the simple cottage where they could spend time together alone in the beauty of the wilderness beat it soundly.

"Yes," Raine said, "the mountain keep, the cottage, then here."

"And Fireside?" Weynild asked, referring to the imperial residence.

"Oh, I don't know, ten, maybe twelve. It's down the list somewhere. 'Amount of sexual activity' plays into the rankings, soo...."

Weynild rolled over on top of her and pinned her. "And I've been to Fireside only a few times, so perhaps you could explain how it ranks as high as ten or twelve?"

A knock on the door interrupted their playful fight. Raine sought to sit up, but Weynild held her fast.

"Come in," she said, staring down into Raine's violet eyes.

Gimle stopped short at the scene greeting her. It was unexpected but not unwelcome to see the silver-haired woman pinning her companion to the bed. And it was evident she was meant to see the scene before her because she had been invited in, so in her very Ha'kan manner, she did not look away or display any discomfiture. Instead, the scholar in her analyzed every detail of the entangled pair with interest.

Raine turned toward her as it was apparent Weynild could sit there all day. "Hello, Gimle."

"Hello, Raine," Gimle said, composed as always. "I hate to disturb you, but a contingency of Dverger has arrived at the palace."

"Dverger?" Raine asked. "Were you expecting any dwarves?"

"No," Gimle said. "They maintain an embassy here in the capital, but they gave no notice and none of these are from that facility. And they seem quite surly, I might add."

"That's a standard state of being for a dwarf, so I'm not sure that's significant."

"Even so," Gimle said calmly, "they're milling about the entrance to the palace and demanding to see you."

"Me? How odd." Raine lifted her head off the pillow and gave a kiss to Weynild. "Sorry, my love. You're the one who appointed me ambassador-at-large. You know I don't care for it, but duty calls."

"Hmmph," the dragon said.

Raine dunked herself in the marble tub of water Weynild had warmed with barely a breath. She dried herself hurriedly, pulled on her armor, and was down the stairs in less than a quarter of an hour.

The group of dwarves milling about was indeed a surly lot, with great axes slung across their backs. The Royal Guard were polite but ill-at-ease, and Raine could sense the tension in the room. Queen Halla stood with Astrid in an alcove, and they were joined by Senta who had been retrieved from the training fields while Raine was getting dressed.

Raine walked directly up to the dwarf in front and spoke to him coldly. "Is there a problem here?"

The Guards were surprised, because the Scinterian was normally very diplomatic and easy-going. Her tone caused them to tighten further, and several rested their hands on the hilt of their swords.

"Yes," the lead dwarf said, his tone just as cold. "I understand there's to be a summit here between the Ha'kan, the Alfar, and the imperials. And I can't help but notice the Dverger were not invited."

"It's hardly a summit," Raine said dismissively. "The Ha'kan and Alfar are merely holding talks. And the imperials come on another matter."

Idonea slipped into the alcove next to Queen Halla. She took one look at the scene before her.

"Oh no," she said.

"And," Raine continued, "if you weren't so fucking thin-skinned about not being invited to the party..."

The Ha'kan were shocked and this was enough to push the enraged dwarf past his point of control. He roared and rushed Raine like a charging bull. Everything seemed to spin out of control, with the dwarves drawing their axes, the Royal Guard lowering their spears, and Raine being tackled with enough force to nearly break the pillar she was shoved against.

"Hold," Idonea commanded, raising her hand and casting the slightest of calming spells. It was not intrusive, a forced compliance, rather just enough to reach out and touch all in the room with the suggestion to briefly stay their hand. "They do this all the time," she said with mild exasperation.

Raine returned the roar and rushed the dwarf just as he had rushed her. She hit him so hard about the shoulders it knocked him backward into his cohorts, who enthusiastically threw him back at Raine. Raine caught him, cuffed him in the head, then threw him to the ground. She jumped on him, and try as he might, he could not free himself.

And then both burst out laughing, the dwarf's deep guffaws echoing off the marble walls. Raine slapped him hard on the shoulders, then jumped to her feet and picked him up by the same. He returned the blow on her shoulders with enough force to break an average person's collar bone, but Raine just grinned.

"Well met, my friend, well met."

No one was quite certain what was going on, but the tension drained from the room, replaced with hesitation. Queen Halla flowed toward them.

"I beg your pardon, your Majesty," Raine said a little sheepishly. "Lorifal and I have something of a tradition."

The name caught the Queen's attention. "Lorifal," she said, "you're a member of the Dwarven High Council, are you not?"

"I am, your Majesty."

Queen Halla gave him a graceful bow. Lorifal's ruddy cheeks grew even ruddier with pleasure at the respectful greeting. The dwarves, although not as refined as the Alfar, were just as proud and the ceremony was not lost on them.

"I confess I'm not here on official business, however." He slapped Raine on the back again and the Ha'kan guards winced at the blow. "I heard Raine was here, and that Feyden might be coming, so I couldn't resist."

"The three of you can't destroy the place like you usually do," Idonea said, coming up to the group.

"By the gods, girl, it's good to see you!" Lorifal said, his eyes bright with pleasure. Impossibly, he grew redder as Idonea leaned down and planted a kiss on his cheek. "This will be another reunion!"

"And if I know Dagna," Raine said, "she'll find a way to come with the imperials in some 'official' capacity."

"And where Dagna goes, her little elf will follow," Idonea said.

"Then we'll all be reunited!" Lorifal exclaimed.

"You're welcome to stay here at the palace, Councilor," Queen Halla proffered.

Lorifal bowed very deeply to the Queen. "Thank you, your Majesty. But we arrived unexpectedly, so we'll not impose. The Dwarven Embassy is right outside the palace gates, so that's more than sufficient."

"I assure you it's no imposition," the Queen replied, "but wherever you're most comfortable."

Raine accompanied Lorifal to the Dwarven Embassy while Idonea was escorted by one of the Royal Guard to the Scholar's Wing of the palace. Idonea was used to the stares of men and women, even the leers from the unsubtle or less sophisticated. But the Ha'kan had a way of looking at one another that was intriguing, a form of eye contact that communicated a myriad of things. There was a general appreciation of the female form, but also a constant evaluation of one another as potential sexual partners. And to Idonea's view, there didn't seem be any negative repercussions from these mental exercises because if it didn't work out, that was probably a temporary situation, and the Ha'kan seemed to enjoy the idea of someone else in bed as much as themselves. It was fascinating for Idonea, who had lived a fairly wanton life but often had to deal with the fall-out from her assignations.

Gimle peered over her spectacles as Idonea entered, and Idonea was privileged to receive one of those intriguing Ha'kan looks.

"Welcome to the Scholar's Wing," Gimle said, "please make yourself at home. Skye is finishing up on the training fields but should be here soon."

Idonea examined the room around her. There were towering bookcases from floor to ceiling, filled with books, scrolls, parchments, and various tomes.

"Your library is impressive," Idonea said.

"Thank you," Gimle said. "We have libraries in every Ha'kan city, but this is the main facility where the originals are kept. The Academy houses a near-duplicate library which maintains copies should anything happen to the books here."

"And what would happen?" Idonea asked curiously. The Ha'kan possessed one of the premiere military forces in all of Arianthem, and the capital was well within Ha'kan territory. It was unlikely it would ever be attacked.

"Some of the younger scholars, my successor in particular, like to blow things up."

"Ah," Idonea said with laughter, "I knew there was a reason I liked Kara."

Gimle adjusted her spectacles. "And when she and Skye get together, which is frequently, they feed off one another. I'm actually thankful Kara has no skill with magic or I'm certain Haldis would have been blown off the map."

"Well, perhaps together we can give Skye a little control over her abilities."

It was a gracious statement from the dark-haired mage. The Ha'kan were not good with magic and very few displayed the gift. Gimle was a rare exception, and she was extremely talented, but she was no match for the magical creature in front of her. Not only had Idonea received extraordinary power from her mother, she had been in training with the greatest wizard in Arianthem for years.

"I welcome your mentoring of Skye," Gimle said, "my magical abilities are defensive in nature: enchanting weapons, utilizing wards and such, to protect Ha'kan troops. Skye needs much more than I can give her. One thing you should know about Skye, though, is that she doesn't learn well by reading. When she first came to the Academy, we thought she was a mediocre student until Kara discovered she learns everything by ear."

"That's right," Idonea said. "The Tavinter are nomads and pass everything along in an oral history."

"Yes. Skye's memory is extraordinary, so Kara often just sits and reads to her."

Idonea leaned back to peer around the corner into a side room that held a comfortable bunk. "Bedtime stories, eh?"

Gimle peered over her spectacles. "Hmm. Yes, that is generally how they end up."

"Oh, I love the Ha'kan," Idonea said to no one in particular.

Skye entered the room and had the impression they were talking about her, which brought a light blush to her cheeks. The blush brought pronounced inspection from Gimle, scrutiny which caused a little knot in Skye's stomach. The willowy First Scholar always affected Skye so, with her cool manner that did not quite hide the sensuality woven into the fabric of her being. And from Kara's off-hand comments, Skye suspected that much of Kara's exploratory nature stemmed directly from the First Scholar, who was simply more discreet than Kara, not necessarily less adventurous.

"So, shall we get your studies going?" Idonea said with a twinkle in her eye. Skye looked at the sultry mage who was barely clothed and seemed to have heat coming off her in waves, then at the fully dressed scholar who exuded cool grace and whose lovely robes clothed her no less enticingly, and sighed.

"I don't know how anyone is supposed to concentrate in these conditions," Skye muttered.

"Ah," Idonea said, "but that's just it. Magic is really about emotion."

This caught Skye's attention.

"And it's been my experience," Idonea continued, "that there's a direct relationship between the strength of the emotion and the effect of the magic. First Scholar?"

Gimle nodded in agreement. "Yes, I've noticed a correlation between intensity of feeling and the power of a spell. The trick, it seems, is controlling the emotion without suppressing it."

"Exactly," Idonea said. "Skye, tell me about your mother."

"What?" Skye said, startled, and her hazel eyes darkened a shade.

"Tell me about your mother," Idonea insisted.

Skye ran her fingers through her hair as Gimle often saw her do when she was uncomfortable or distressed.

"She was beautiful," Skye began, "and strong and brave. She was very kind, funny, good at everything, but humble."

The reserved scholar felt a tightening in her throat. Skye's gaze had grown distant and she smiled sadly as she thought of her mother. Truly, Skye could have been describing herself, but was too unassuming to draw the comparison.

"Tell me what happened to your mother," Idonea said, her voice taking on a hypnotic quality.

And Skye seemed to be hypnotized, so lost in memory was she. "I thought she was sick, I thought that she had died from illness."

"But that's not what happened, is it?" Idonea said quietly, prompting a glance from Gimle who thought it a harsh question.

"No," Skye said, now fully elsewhere. Her tone grew harder, filled with conviction. "No, she was killed by Reaper Shards who sensed her magic and came for her."

Gimle watched the parade of emotions on Skye's face as the girl was clearly reliving, or at least imagining, her mother's death.

"They poisoned her with their evil, and she couldn't recover."

Skye was completely lost in thought now, utterly distracted, and Gimle was stunned when Idonea threw her hand back and launched a ball of pure fire at Skye. She was even more stunned when Skye casually raised her hand and stopped the ball of fire, deflecting it off at an angle so that it caromed from a wall then landed on Gimle's desk. Fortunately, the flame had dissipated much of its energy from impact and redirection, so it only started a small fire on the paperwork there. Gimle grabbed the bucket of flame retardant she kept handy for Kara's mishaps and dumped the powder on the blaze, extinguishing it.

Idonea's dark eyelashes flicked to Gimle. "Sorry about that."

"I'm used to it," Gimle said, gathering herself. "And we do have another set at the Academy."

Skye was more than stunned, she was astonished. But Idonea did not even seem surprised.

"Skye, what were you thinking about when you blocked that fire?"

"I was thinking that I wished I could have protected my mother."

"Do you even know the spell that you just cast?"

"No," Skye said in disbelief, shaking her head.

"It was a ward of protection," Idonea said, "a spell you didn't even have to know to use. And that," she said with growing seriousness, "is your gift from Isleif."

"Isleif?" Skye said.

"Your great-grandfather was, and still is, immensely powerful. But that's not what made him the greatest wizard Arianthem has ever known. He feels magic. And he lets it flow through him without resistance, without obstruction. There are few that have that gift. But what separates even those few is the ability to control that magic and not let it control you. It's what he taught me," she finished gently.

"You feel magic?" Skye asked. "Like that?"

"Oh, yes," Idonea said, "although I'm not certain I could cast a spell I've never even seen."

"But I think I have seen that before. Gimle, didn't you use that against the Reaper Shards?"

"Yes," Gimle said, "not the same spell, but one similar. That was very good, Skye."

The corner of Skye's mouth tugged upward. This was much better than reading. Actually performing magic was exciting, even if she had no idea what she was doing.

Idonea examined Skye for signs of fatigue. From what Gimle had told her, Skye was not used to casting spells and would have to build up her endurance to do so consistently. But Skye seemed fine, so she proceeded.

"Gimle told me you've experimented with a true invisibility spell, not one based on illusion magic. Could you show me this spell?"

Skye looked at Gimle uncertainly. The First Scholar had forbidden her to use the spell because despite her vast knowledge, she had never seen or heard such a thing. Many mages were able to cast spells that influenced the mind, but Gimle was highly resistant to this type of spell, so it was not an illusion. Others were able to use enchanted artifacts to pass through the various realms, giving the perception of appearing and disappearing without actually doing so.

This was something different.

"You may use the spell under Idonea's direction," Gimle said. She picked up a scroll and set it in front of Skye, then changed her mind. "No, not that one." She picked up another, less rare document and traded it out. "Just in case."

"And one more thing," Idonea said. She waved her hand about the room and a cube of blue light enclosed the three of them. "A barrier of sorts, just in case."

Skye frowned. They weren't doing much for her confidence. She looked at the scroll in front of her, trying to remember what she had been thinking about last time, in light of Idonea's recent instruction regarding emotion. She had been thinking about being Tavinter, about her people's gift of camouflage. Specifically, she had been thinking about blending into the forest until she was completely unseen...

The scroll disappeared. Idonea did not react beyond the slightest lifting of one fine eyebrow. She stepped forward, reached out, and picked up the invisible object. She could feel its weight, its outline, even the texture of the paper. But it could not be seen.

"Can you bring it back?" Idonea asked.

Before she would not have been certain how, but now Skye thought about coming out of hiding in the forest. And the scroll reappeared.

"Amazing," Idonea murmured, "it's what Isleif suspected."

"Isleif knows of this spell?" Gimle asked. "We have nothing about it in our archives."

"He'd heard rumor of this spell, long, long ago. He even experimented with it, but had no success. He wondered if it was because he used Light Magic and Dark Magic equally."

"Isleif uses Dark Magic? Isn't that dangerous?" Skye asked.

"All magic is dangerous, little one. And contrary to popular belief, Dark Magic, or 'Black Magic' isn't necessarily evil. It simply springs from a different source. And the creatures from the void, who generally are evil, have a great affinity towards it. Which is why it usually manifests as evil. But trust me," Idonea said thoughtfully, "there are creatures of light that are just as dangerous."

"So magic is essentially neutral?" Gimle asked. "Both Light and Dark?"

"Hmm, yes and no," Idonea answered. "Both are powerfully influenced by their source, but it's a tendency rather than fate. Dark Magic can be used for good, and Light Magic can be used for evil."

"And you use both?"

"Yes," Idonea said. "Dragons are filled with Dark Magic, so my dragon blood makes me gifted in that aspect. But Dark Magic is not appropriate for every situation, so I train in Light Magic as well. It was Isleif who helped me understand this."

"So, this is a spell of Light Magic?" Skye asked.

"Most definitely," Idonea said, "it appears you're bending light itself to make the object disappear, so it's Light Magic in its purest form. Which is probably why no one has ever been able to use it. It requires someone with enormous power and natural ability, and someone who has never used Dark Magic."

"Well I don't know about that first part," Skye said, chewing on her lip, "but I don't think I've ever used Dark Magic."

"Although this is contrary to the advice I usually give, I don't think you ever should." Idonea saw Skye beginning to show the fatigue she was watching for. She waved her hand and the blue cube of light surrounding them disappeared. "I think you should rest for a while."

Gimle was also aware of Skye's sudden exhaustion. "Why don't you go lie down in that bunk in there?"

"Thank you," Skye said. She walked into the side room, took off her shoes, and collapsed in the bed. It smelled of frankincense and juniper. Skye breathed in the wonderful aroma; it smelled exactly like Gimle. She would probably have wonderful dreams about the First Scholar.

Idonea examined the scroll in her hand. There was a trace of misgiving in her voice.

"Under normal circumstances, I would never advise someone to focus on only one type of magic. But Isleif felt Skye's gift must remain pure."

"I can understand the danger of using pure Black Magic," Gimle said, "but what danger is there in pure Light Magic?"

"It's probably just an allegory, but there's a saying that the gods can grow jealous and return for their children. Practitioners of Dark Magic are warned that Nótt, the Goddess of Night, will come for them."

Idonea turned her gaze from scroll to the already sleeping figure half-visible through the door.

"I fear that Baldr will come for that one."

The Ha'kan worshipped Sjöfn, the Goddess of love, above all deities. But Baldr, son of the Allfather and God of Light, was also revered, so Gimle understood Idonea's words.

"The blue light, the spell you cast before Skye turned the scroll invisible. That wasn't a barrier spell."

"No," Idonea said, "it was a type of absorption spell, a cloak if you will. Isleif taught it to me with the specific intent I surround Skye with it if she was doing anything extraordinary. It keeps other magical beings from sensing her."

"It keeps the Reaper Shards away," Gimle stated more directly.

"Exactly," Idonea said. "Isleif began developing it after Skye's mother, Isolde, was killed. It's a difficult spell and I can't maintain it for very long. But it'll hide her for the time being, until we can get her skill developed. We just have to get her to generate some emotion."

"I really don't think that will be a problem."

Gimle's tone of voice, so matter of fact, yet with that slight, erotic edge that all Ha'kan possessed, made the corner of Idonea's mouth turn up. Skye had let slip she occasionally shared the bed of the First General, divulging how sexually overwhelming the fully mature Ha'kan women could be. Clearly it would not be long before Skye was sharing the bed of the First Scholar as well.

"I knew there was more than one reason Isleif sent Skye to the Ha'kan."

"Hmm," Gimle said, "perhaps multiple reasons. You know, the Ha'kan are not good with magic. There's a story from the distant past of one gifted young woman who was very powerful, but had no control over her abilities, and no one to help her. And so, she was imprisoned."

"That doesn't sound very much like the Ha'kan."

"You misunderstand. She was confined to a tower that was luxuriously furnished and staffed with a full complement of Priestesses. You see," Gimle said, turning to Idonea and peering over her glasses, "the only way this woman could control her power was by having sex at least three or four times a day."

"Now that sounds more like the Ha'kan," Idonea said, liking this version of the story very much.

"The sexual exertion, the release, seemed to 'take the edge off,' so to speak," Gimle continued, "and she was able to live a long and happy life."

Idonea thought about her conversation with her mother the night before, about the seeming relationship between sexual escapades and magical ability. That seemed to be making more and more sense.

"Again, it seems Isleif may have sent Skye here for many reasons."

Chapter 3

The week passed quickly. Skye now looked forward to her lessons with the First Scholar and Idonea, and she began making slow but steady progress. Gimle was astonished at Skye's skill and even Idonea, who had spent years with Isleif, was impressed. Skye was oblivious to her unusual proficiency and simply had fun blowing things up.

The dwarves settled into their embassy but spent many hours on the Ha'kan training fields brawling with Raine. It seemed less training than entertainment for them, and Senta was certain someone was going to be decapitated by the swings of those great axes, but no mishaps occurred. Weynild, as was her custom, spent much of her time alone, or perched upon the parapet of the castle, her gold eyes scanning the horizon. They would drift down to gaze fondly upon her Scinterian, who would sense the attention and look upward with adoration, then the dragon would return to her vigil.

And so, the few days flew by, and it was with great anticipation that Queen Halla received word, relayed from a Tavinter ranger, that the Alfar were but hours away. The Ha'kan contingency deployed to join them had already done so, and from what the scout reported, the Alfar, as usual, were in full, ceremonial procession.

The Ha'kan lined the streets as the Alfar marched eight abreast into the capital. They were glorious in their elven armor, its polished gold and green surface gleaming in the sun. The soldiers marched straight ahead, looking neither right or left, their expressions impassive. The Alfar Ambassador was in the middle of the procession, dressed in the shimmering robes for which the Alfar were famous. She wore a jeweled circlet on her head, simple but elegant, and her long hair was braided down her back. Her features were refined, her almond-shaped eyes exotic. The Ha'kan who appreciated beauty above all else, appreciated her.

And although Maeva's expression was as impassive as that of her troops, it was hard not be impressed with the Ha'kan capital. It was an architectural wonder, its serpentine streets somehow flowing with the grace and loveliness of the Ha'kan themselves. And the fact that those streets were lined with stunning women of all descriptions, some dressed in robes, some dressed in armor, some dressed in casual wear, only added to that loveliness.

Queen Halla stood at the top of the steps, flanked by her First Scholar, her First General, and the High Priestess. All wore their official ceremonial clothing, Gimle in her graceful Scholar's robes, Astrid in the exquisite robes of the Ministry, and Senta in her armor, the Ha'kan eagle slightly raised on her chest. And Halla wore the royal vestments, cut so perfectly to reveal curves, to allow a glimpse of that wondrous cleavage.

To Halla's right stood Dallan and her staff, mirroring both the positions and, unconsciously, the mannerisms of their mentors. They also wore the vestments of their castes and positions, the only difference being Dallan, who, still a member of the Warrior caste, wore polished armor like Senta's, but slightly modified to indicate her royal position. Skye stood next to Dallan, wearing a pristine version of the stylish leather armor of the Tavinter Rangers.

To Halla's left stood the dwarves, whom the Queen had invited to be present when the Alfar arrived. The dwarves were greatly pleased by this honor extended to them and had dressed for the occasion. The dwarves might not have been as elegant or beautiful as the Ha'kan and Alfar, but no one could mine or smith better, and the results of those skills were fully on display. Although Lorifal barely came to her elbow, Senta nudged him in the shoulder.

"Now that," she said approvingly, "is armor."

Lorifal's cheeks went ruddy with pleasure, and he shifted the great ax on his shoulder.

The procession entered the palace gate and the elven soldiers began peeling off in military precision, four to each side, where they fell into ranks facing the middle. The Ambassador proceeded down the center of the ranks, stopped at the bottom of the stairs, and dismounted her horse. As the Alfar put great symbolism on all greetings, it had been formally arranged that Queen Halla would descend downward to the first landing while the Ambassador ascended upward to the same, and the two would meet halfway.

Weynild observed the arrival from the terrace. Idonea joined her at her side.

"Who's that?"

Idonea looked to her mother. Her tone was even as always, but there was an underlying intensity that attracted Idonea's attention. She followed her mother's gaze to the young woman who accompanied Maeva, the one who was now being assisted from her horse by an elven soldier.

"Ah," Idonea said, "from what I understand that's Maeva's most prized possession. That's the heir to the House of Storr, the one whom the imperials come for."

"Where's Raine?" Weynild asked, her intensity not diminishing a whit.

Idonea was curious and a little concerned by this seemingly unrelated question.

"I'm not certain. She said she would be out in a moment. Why?"

"I need to be near her when she sees that girl."

Raine pushed through the stained-glass doors and onto the terrace. She was a little disappointed to have missed the grand entrance because the Alfar so loved a parade. She moved to the stone railing, looked down, and time seemed to stop. A look of cold fury appeared on her features, the blue and gold markings on her back, shoulders and forearms rose to the surface, and her hands went to the swords on her back. And the swords would have flashed outward were she not suddenly encased in solid rock.

"You will stay your hand," Weynild hissed, the hiss not from anger but because the dragon in her was present in all but appearance. She had come up behind Raine and immobilized her in a crushing embrace. And Raine's anger spiked even more, for Weynild never used her great strength against her other than in play. Her breathing came out in ragged gasps, partially because of her fury, and partially because of the enormous force being used to restrain her.

"That girl is Arlanian," Raine said, biting off each word.

"No," Weynild said, "she's not. Any Arlanian blood in her is from an ancestor centuries ago."

"You know that doesn't matter," Raine said through gritted teeth. "You know what a single drop of blood will do to her."

"Look," Weynild said, directing her attention to the scene below.

Raine looked, and saw the elven guards imprisoning the girl, saw the Alfar Ambassador gaze on the helpless woman-child with cool possession, her sexual toy. It enraged her and Weynild feared she would have to break Raine's bones to keep her in check.

"I see!" Raine said.

"You don't," Weynild insisted, "Look again!"

And Raine obeyed the command, trying to calm herself. And as she did so, she became aware of how gently the elven guards treated the raven-haired girl, how they looked on her fondly and with respect. And the cold, fierce warriors suddenly seemed less her imprisoners than her protectors.

Weynild felt the subtle shift in Raine. "Look at Maeva."

And Raine did, noting the even subtler signs she had missed before, how Maeva reached down and brushed the young woman's cheek with her hand, barely a gesture, but a public display of affection almost unheard of for the Alfar, let alone their supremely reserved Ambassador.

"Maeva is in love with her," Raine said slowly.

"And look at the girl," Weynild commanded.

And again Raine obeyed, looking down at the small creature who gazed up at Maeva with those stunning, sapphire eyes, her expression joyful, curious, and excited.

"The girl returns that love," Raine said at last, the tension draining from her body. Weynild tempered her embrace, not releasing her, but instead just pulling her closer.

"Yes. And that girl is the reason Maeva has softened her stance towards the Empire, because she believes her to be fully human."

As important as this fact was, it didn't seem very important to Raine right now, so Weynild continued her persuasion.

"And, barring yourself, can you think of any greater protector for the girl than the future Directorate of the Alfar?"

Raine relaxed so completely at this question and its obvious answer that Weynild now supported her full weight, which was far easier than restraining her.

"No," Raine admitted, drained. "I can't. I'm sorry."

Weynild buried her face in her lover's hair, kissing her.

"There's no need for apologies between you and me, ever. I knew you would react that way the instant you saw her. I'm wondering, however," Weynild said, stroking the still-visible markings on Raine's arms, "when you became so strong."

The sensual undertone in Weynild's voice was back, and between that and the exquisite, feathery touch on her arm, Raine was instantly lost to her love. She took one last look at the scene below, then turned to the dragon.

"In two decades, this is our first fight, so to speak," she said, a trace of mischief in her voice. "Do you know that the Ha'kan handle almost all conflict by having sex?"

"They're a very wise people," Weynild said, taking her love by the hand and leading her back through the stained-glass doors.

The participants in the ceremony below were oblivious to the drama occurring above, and Idonea joined Lorifal on the upper landing. Queen Halla was descending the stairs with her inner circle as Maeva was ascending with her immediate staff.

"Where's Raine?" Lorifal whispered.

"She and my mother had a bit of a spat and well, you know how they are."

Lorifal grinned. He could only imagine what was going on up there right now, and he was lost in that pleasant reverie for a few minutes, unaware of the ceremony before him.

Queen Halla and Maeva arrived on the landing simultaneously, a feat which Halla had carefully arranged and which the elves took as coincidence designating good fortune. Although Maeva was technically only an Ambassador and in an official sense, worthy of a lesser greeting, the Queen gave her the deep curtsy of one ruling leader to another. Maeva understood the acknowledgment and recognition of her future position within the Alfar, and the gesture pleased her. Unlike the imperials, who had sought to impress her with their arrogance, the Ha'kan were gracious and skilled diplomats. Maeva thought these talks would go far better than those with the Empire.

"Welcome to Haldis, Ambassador. Both I and my staff greet you."

Maeva's eyes went to the lovely, bespectacled First Scholar, lingered on the sultry, elegant High Priestess, then moved to the First General who loomed over all of them.

"My, you grow them big here."

It was a test of sorts, an ambiguous statement that could be taken as benign or as insult. But Senta's eyes merely twinkled with warmth and good humor as the Queen sent her First General a mild glance that would have melted the ice on Mount Alfheim.

"Yes," she said smoothly, "we do."

And it delighted Maeva, although none of this appeared on her face. The Ha'kan had mastered subtle intricacies to which the imperials were oblivious. Halla gestured for her to join her side and walk with her, and the two started back up the stairs.

"I must comment on the beauty of the Ha'kan capital," Maeva said, "and may I extend an invitation to you and your staff to visit the Alfar capital sometime soon, so that I may return your hospitality."

This was an early and significant concession as most outsiders were banned from Alfar lands. "It's my understanding," Halla said delicately, "that a new Directorate will be announced before too long. Perhaps said visit would coincide with such an event so the Ha'kan could pay respects to the new Head of State."

"I believe the new Head of State would like that," Maeva said, again appreciating the smooth diplomacy of the Ha'kan Queen.

They reached the upper landing and Halla guided Maeva to a group of younger Ha'kan.

"Ambassador, this is my daughter, Dallan."

Maeva would have known the Princess with no introduction, for she had her mother's flashing dark eyes and lustrous dark hair. She wore her hair shorter and was not as voluptuous as the Queen, but she was unmistakably Halla's daughter.

"I'm pleased to meet you, Ambassador," Dallan said, bowing formally, "and welcome to the Ha'kan capital. I and my staff are at your service."

Maeva glanced to the other young women, and it was evident which role each would play in the future. Evident until she came to the one standing between the future First General and the future High Priestess. She examined the young woman with the fair hair, the light tan skin, the hazel eyes. She was shorter than most of her cohorts and of much smaller build. Slender, almost elven, but lacking the uniquely shaped eyes and slightly pointed ears. She was definitely not Ha'kan. Dallan stepped forward.

"This is Skye, ruler of the Tavinter. She's also head of the Tavinter Rangers, who ride with the Ha'kan."

"Ah, yes," Maeva said thoughtfully. "The Tavinter, once bitter enemies of the Ha'kan, now fierce allies. It'll be most interesting to hear how that came about."

Skye's cheeks turned a fetching shade of crimson. It was a long story, involving her father's assassination, a convoluted plot by the Garmlain to frame the Tavinter, and a three-year guerilla war between the Tavinter and Ha'kan. But most of it came about by her spending almost every night in the arms of one of the women that stood on this platform, and many nights, more than one of them.

"Ambassador," Skye said, bowing stiffly.

Maeva enjoyed looking at the girl. Unlike the Ha'kan who were so possessed and self-assured, this one could barely meet her gaze. And something about her seemed familiar, especially when Maeva glanced back to the Princess and the future First General. Something about their positions and their relative sizes...

"We've met before," Skye blurted out, and Rika covered her eyes in exasperation. Dallan's self-assurance evaporated under her mother's sudden scrutiny. "I did tell you about that, mother," Dallan muttered, "eventually."

"Yes," Halla said, "eventually."

The miniature drama she was creating entertained Maeva. "And where did we meet?"

"On the imperial highway," Skye said, "when you were first coming down the mountain."

The puzzle pieces locked into place. "You were with Raine," she said. Two of them had been hooded and disguised, but Maeva had an eye for detail and an excellent memory. This Tavinter was lovely and had a way of moving that reminded Maeva of a forest animal. These three had accompanied the Scinterian when she had boldly stopped the entire Alfar procession.

Apparently, the Queen had quite a memory herself. "Yes," she said drily, addressing Dallan. "I remember it well. You were on 'vacation.'"

The gentle scolding was good-humored and Dallan took it so. "I've apologized a thousand times for that, your Majesty."

The Queen brushed her daughter's cheek. "It's fortunate for you that you're so charming." She touched Maeva lightly on the elbow, then gestured to the contingency of dwarves. "And we have some unexpected but welcome guests."

Maeva moved to the Dverger, stopping before one in particular. She examined him at length, a mild vexation on her face that bordered on scorn.

"Lorifal," she said at last. "Now it's assured my brother will spend most of his time here inebriated."

"So Feyden is coming," Lorifal said, hope on his ruddy features.

"Of course, he's coming. As much as he'd like to spend his days cavorting with you and Raine, I do demand him to attend to his duties."

"Yes," Lorifal said, not hiding his own sarcasm, "he's mentioned that a few times."

Halla would have been disturbed at the adversarial nature of the interaction, but Raine had warned her that Lorifal and Maeva always acted so, that both were most comfortable baiting one another and in fact enjoyed it. Raine had been adamant that if they were rude to one another, it was a good sign, and if they were not, then something was terribly awry.

"Speaking of which," Maeva said, "where is Raine?"

Lorifal cleared his throat, shifted his ax, looked at the ground, then cleared his throat again, making it imminently clear what Raine was most likely doing at that moment. He flailed about, then looked to the woman to his left for help. Maeva turned to her and was taken aback that she had not seen her before. This woman cared little for formality for, unlike the carefully chosen attire of the Ha'kan, was dressed in robes more appropriate for a boudoir. Maeva was not certain how the clothing was staying in place as the bodice of the dress started somewhere around her naval. Beautiful full breasts threatened to spill from their sparse confinement, just as laughter threatened to spill from her full red lips. She was bewitching, and Maeva solidified her resolve against her just as she did against all she was strongly attracted to, at the same time mentally leaving her options open. Although she would allow none to touch her young companion, she did not always hold herself to the same high standard of fidelity.

Lorifal instantly regretted his unspoken plea for help. Although he and Maeva had a history of banter, Idonea had a way about her that could destroy nations. And her irreverence might strike the Alfar Ambassador as disrespectful, even a grave insult. He hoped that for once she would come down on the side of tact and restraint.

She did not.

"I'm fairly certain Raine is still in bed with my mother."

All heads turned at the ribald and inappropriate comment, its unsuitable content highlighted by the staid ceremony surrounding it. Idonea merely gazed expectantly at the Alfar Ambassador. Contrary to what most thought, although Maeva's arrogance permeated her entire being, its display was carefully regulated, used more as a tool than a form of expression. And although she could have returned this careless, offhand remark with a withering response, the most important part of the sentence is what caught her attention.

"You are the dragon's daughter," she murmured.

Idonea extended her hand. "Yes. My name is Idonea." And although the greeting was extraordinary in its lack of formality, Maeva took the hand. Queen Halla stepped forward. "Ambassador, Idonea is the daughter of Talan'alaith'illaria and the protégé of Isleif."

"I see," Maeva said, still holding the hand, marveling at the unexpected softness of the skin and the warmth of the touch. Her eyes drifted back to the breasts, imagining how soft that skin must be as well. The woman's identity explained the dark magical energy that swirled around her, filled with particles that were neither positive nor negative in origin, but rather charged with a primordial sexual energy. The dark, laughing eyes did not waver.

Maeva released the hand. "I'm pleased to make your acquaintance," the Ambassador said formally, but it was the most informal of formal greetings, surprising even her own staff. "And I look forward to your company."

Queen Halla led the Ambassador and her entourage up the marble staircase into the palace where they would be settled into the guest wing. Lorifal released his breath, the breath he had been holding since he had first made the horrible mistake of turning to Idonea for help.

"I'll tell you right now, girl," the dwarf said, "you don't want to get tangled up with that one. She's a spider with a web that extends across all of Arianthem."

"You know," Idonea said, watching the departing dignitaries, "I had a pet spider as a child. A hideous little creature I kept in a jar. I had it for months, then it escaped into the house."

"And what happened to it?" Lorifal asked.

"My mother crushed it," she said, watching the dignitaries disappear.

CHAPTER 4

The Queen had planned a dinner for the Alfar, although not the formal one that would be held once the imperials arrived. Although the imperials were not a party to the treaty negotiations between the Alfar and Ha'kan, Talan did not feel such an opportunity should be wasted. It was unusual for representatives of the proposed alliances to all be in one place, let alone such a favorable place as the Ha'kan capital. Talan had approached the Queen early on and privately suggested it was possible that both the imperials and dwarves would arrive with the Alfar, a prospect Halla had thought extremely unlikely given the rivalry and discord that existed between these nations. But Halla had assured Talan that, should that occur, the Ha'kan would play host to all of them. And as the dragon queen had predicted, all were coming to the table, leading Halla to wonder how much of that had been by Talan's design.

But that feast was days away. And in the meantime, the Ha'kan Queen and the Ambassador would discuss an alliance between their people, and there would be pageantry to exemplify and celebrate the skills of both nations. And tonight, there would be a very special gathering, one organized in a distinctly Ha'kan manner.

The evening started early in the informal dining room of the palace. The Queen had a personal, semi-formal dining room which was arranged much like a normal space for eating: a rectangular table where she and her staff, as well as Dallan and her staff, would sit down to visit and share a meal or celebration. The formal dining room was immense and would be used for the meal once the imperials arrived.

But the room in which they dined this evening was a Ha'kan gathering place, and it was carefully arranged to create a feeling of intimacy and openness, two characteristics contrary everywhere except Ha'kan culture. Plush, circular couches surrounded round tables, creating little islands throughout the room. Such an arrangement in any other social structure might have led to cliques and isolated pockets of conversation, but it never did so with the Ha'kan. The cushioned seats were all close enough that one could lean over from one island to another and join whatever interaction was occurring there, so that the isles were more like links in a chain rather than separate entities.

And initial seating was not assigned; rather it was the responsibility of the High Priestess and her staff to see that all were engaged and enjoying themselves. With a normal gathering, consisting of nothing but Ha'kan, this was an effortless task. With the current group, Astrid felt it might prove more challenging, and had enlisted the help of Dallan and Lifa. She watched the two young women with pride, Dallan so charming and funny, and Lifa so lovely and warm, as they placed all around them at ease.

Maeva had entered with several of her staff and introduced Edwenil, another member of elven royalty who shared the icy beauty and imperious manner of the Ambassador, and who seemed to be somewhere high in the elven hierarchy. It was difficult to tease out the complicated relationships of the Alfar, but it seemed Edwenil might rank somewhere just below Feyden. Maeva was also accompanied by Faelon, her chief of security, a handsome, arrogant male whose eyes continually scanned the room. Maeva's personal assistant, Melwen, hovered about Maeva's elbow, unfortunately blocking the path between the adjacent islands until Maeva, with some irritation, ordered him to sit down. Queen Halla and Astrid sat with the Ambassador, engaging in graceful small talk until even Melwen calmed down.

"We look forward to your exhibition," the Queen said. "It's well known how skilled the archers of the Alfar are."

"The finest in all of Arianthem," Faelon pronounced. It was indeterminate if his words were deliberately or unintentionally insulting, but Halla graciously let them pass either way.

"I'm sure we'll enjoy it," she said. "And perhaps you would like a tour of the palace tomorrow?" she asked, turning to Maeva.

"I would enjoy that very much," Maeva said with a scathing glance at Faelon. She made a note to berate him later for his uncouth manner and was tempted to do so now, but her attention was drawn to a figure who had just entered and stood partially in shadow in the doorway. A surge of desire spread throughout Maeva's body as she examined the lithe frame, the sculpted arms revealed by the sleeveless tunic, the chiseled features that Sjöfn herself had carved into flesh. The dark blue eyes scanned the room, then settled upon her. Raine gave a brief bow of respect, then started down the few steps into the room.

And then it was not merely Maeva's eyes upon her, but every eye in the room as all felt the magnetism of the mythical creature in their midst. The Alfar, seated about the room, shifted on their cushions, some to get a better look, some to dissipate the heat that was building in the lower parts of their bodies. Male and female were equally affected, and not one was immune. The Ha'kan seemed the most appreciative but least affected, perhaps because they did not resist the magnetism but rather just enjoyed the sensation this woman produced in them so effortlessly.

"Raine!" Skye exclaimed as Raine approached. "Lorifal was just telling stories about you!"

With a little effort on Dallan's part, she, Skye, and Rika had infiltrated a group of dwarves, which had quickly become the rowdiest group in the room. Senta and Gimle were off having serious discussions with a group of elves and several of Senta's staff. Kara and Lifa were entertaining a mixed group of Ha'kan, dwarves, and elves, and the Queen was entertaining Maeva and her immediate staff. But this group appeared to be having the most fun.

"This group looks like nothing but trouble," Raine commented.

"Oh, you wound me lass," Lorifal said, well into his third round of drinks.

"Is that your anise liqueur?" Raine asked, nodding toward his glass.

"By the gods, yes. And the Ha'kan have perfected this drink as none other."

"They are skilled," Raine agreed. "And Kara, the future First Scholar, has been working on the ingredients for a perfect amber sting."

Raine was getting ready to move on, to make her obligatory social rounds, when the tail-end of Rika's conversation caught her ear. Rika, who could drink almost anyone under the table, was heartily challenged by this group of dwarves. They were a rambunctious quartet downing mead with abandon.

"So," Rika said curiously, glancing around at the all-male contingency, "there are female dwarves, are there not?"

Raine winced and the laughter of the group stopped.

"I AM female," said the dwarf whom Rika was addressing. She stood belligerently, albeit unsteadily while both Dallan and Skye looked on in dismay. Rika's expression was one of alarm. Although she could be irreverent and even crude, she was never rude. She would have given anything to reel those words back in. She was so shocked at how the situation was unraveling she did not even move to defend herself from the oncoming blow.

She did not have to as Raine stepped between them and easily caught both the flailing fist and unsteady dwarf. With a gentle push, she sent the dwarf back onto the cushions behind her.

"Gruna," Raine said as if addressing a child, "do you remember the tavern in Kollsvik, the Rotten Egg or whatever that atrocious place was called?"

"Yes, yes. The Rotten Eye."

Raine frowned. That was even worse than she remembered.

"Do you remember saying, quite loudly if I recall, that you couldn't tell the difference between the sons and daughters of men?"

Gruna smiled at the remembrance, then realized the point Raine was making. "That's different," she protested.

"It's not," Raine said, "it's exactly the same. Although I believe Rika's insult was unintentional while yours was deliberate."

Gruna again smiled at the memory. "That was a fun brawl."

"Hmm. Yes, but there'll be no brawling here," Raine said firmly.

"Don't worry, Raine," Lorifal said, interjecting himself into the conversation. He would have interjected himself into the potential fight, but he knew Raine had things well in hand. "We'll act civilized." He glared at Gruna.

"Sorry," Gruna muttered.

"You have my apologies as well," Rika said, addressing the dwarf, "I'm appalled I said that." And Gruna just grinned, because the wrath of a dwarf could dissipate as quickly as it had risen, leaving no trace behind.

"Good," Raine said, "we're all friends again." She saw that Senta was uneasy, watching the scene unfold. "I'm going to go soothe the concerns of your First General."

"Please don't tell her what I said," Rika said.

"From what I've seen of Senta, I won't have to," Raine said, "she'll get the story from you directly."

Rika furrowed her brow. "No," she said, nodding in Skye's direction, "she'll get it from her."

"'Tis true," Skye muttered, "I can't hide anything from her."

"You can't hide anything from anyone," Dallan said.

Raine made her way across the room to Senta, who greeted her warmly by clasping her forearm.

"Everything all right over there?"

"Oh yes," Raine assured her, "typical dwarven shenanigans. They've promised to behave, and Lorifal will maintain the peace."

Senta looked over to the young Ha'kan. There was clearly more to this story than Raine was letting on, and she gazed pointedly at Skye. Skye looked away and Senta made a note to speak to the three later.

"Things seem to be going well thus far," Raine said, perusing the room. Everyone appeared to be mingling in a relaxed manner.

"Yes, although I'm surprised that the eyes of the Alfar Ambassador haven't burned a hole right through you since they've been focused on nothing else since you walked in the room."

"I will say that's why I enjoy the company of the Ha'kan," Raine replied.

"The Ha'kan stare at you as much as anyone else."

"Yes, but you all stare at one another the same way," Raine said, "so at least I blend in."

"You don't blend in anywhere, my friend," Senta said, laughing, "but I'm thankful you feel comfortable with us."

Raine lowered her voice. "Who's the woman with Maeva?"

Senta also lowered her voice. "I believe her name is Edwenil, and for the record, her eyes haven't left you either."

"Thank you for that status update. Do you know anything about her?"

As the security of the event, and in fact, the entire conference, was her responsibility, Senta knew exactly who was present.

"Edwenil was Maeva's chief competitor for the position of Directorate. When it became apparent that Maeva would easily obtain the position, Edwenil wisely bowed out of the contest and allied herself with Maeva. She's become her staunch supporter and a close friend, a boon for Maeva since Edwenil's lineage rivals hers."

"So, two ancient houses aligned."

"Exactly," Senta said.

"And the two men?"

Raine stood with her back to the Queen's circle, but Senta was facing them and could easily see over Raine's head. She continued to speak in low tones.

"The man dressed in the simple tunic is Maeva's personal assistant, Melwen. From my brief interaction with him, he's typical Alfar in that he's cold and arrogant. But he's also extremely intelligent, competent, and has a grasp of facts and figures that's daunting. He's also fiercely loyal to Maeva."

"And the other?"

"That's Faelon, Maeva's chief of security. He's egotistical even for an Alfar. When he arrived, I tried to coordinate security efforts with him, but he insisted the Alfar could take care of their own. He's been dismissive since he got here."

"So, a lively group all around?"

"Exactly," Senta said, appreciating Raine's dry summary.

"Then perhaps it's time I rescue your Queen and High Priestess?"

Senta chuckled. "I'm sure they would be indebted to you."

Raine approached the Queen's circle and Halla looked to her with that Ha'kan look that made Raine smile, and a degree of fondness of which Maeva took silent note. Her intelligence sources said that Raine had twice saved

Halla's daughter from certain death, and the bond between the Scinterian and the Ha'kan was evident.

"Your Majesty," Raine said, bowing low. "And High Priestess." Raine turned to Maeva. "Ambassador," she said, bowing just as low.

"Raine," Maeva said, "it's good to see you again. Are you following up to see that I keep my word?"

Maeva had given Raine a guarantee that she would approach negotiations with the imperials in good faith.

"Of course not," Raine said, "I trust you implicitly."

Maeva's eyes drifted down the length of Raine's frame. "That could be a mistake in certain matters."

There was a twinkle in Raine's blue eyes. "Then let us hope I have the judgment to separate business from pleasure." She turned back to Queen Halla. "With the Ha'kan that's in vain, because they're always one and the same."

Both Edwenil and Faelon were shocked at the exchange between the Ambassador and Raine. Although the hint had been indirect, it was positively heated for one referred to as the "ice queen."

"Raine," Astrid said, "The tunic you're wearing is lovely. I've never seen one like it."

"It's a very ancient design," Raine explained, "one that hasn't been seen in Arianthem in over 300 years. These are the vestments of my mother's people."

Astrid examined the clothing with wonder. It was dark blue, but shifted in the light, appearing almost purple at times. Multi-color thread was woven into the fabric with such care it did not change the overall color of the clothing but gave the shimmering appearance of tiny rainbows as Raine moved. It was gorgeous, worthy of the people it represented.

"I don't mean to presume, and please tell me if my request is out of line. But would you be willing to share this design with our clothiers?" Astrid asked. "We wouldn't be so disrespectful to copy it directly, but perhaps modify it for our fashions?"

"My mother's people are no longer here," Raine said quietly, "but I've often wished that the Ha'kan had been the first to discover them, because they might still be here today. Since I'm all that's left to speak for them, I would be honored if the Ha'kan wore these vestments."

Something in what Raine had just said triggered a thought, and she turned to Maeva, changing the subject.

"And where's your young companion? The heir to the House of Storr?"

Maeva's wariness spiked and a wall came down between them.

"Her name is Kiren," Maeva said carefully. "She was very tired from the journey so I thought she should rest this evening."

Raine assessed her for a long moment. It was a unique experience for Maeva to be so examined, to be filleted, scaled, skinned, and cleaned by a mere look, especially when she was the one used to conducting such an examination.

"She seems happy," Raine said. But there were a thousand meanings in those three words, a hundred different levels of intensity, an observation, an edict, a warning, and other things that were unfathomable.

"Yes," Maeva said, "Kiren is unique for an imperial. She's brilliant, a talented artist, musician, and scholar. She speaks numerous languages and in fact was instrumental in translating during negotiations with the Deep Miners."

The thought of this brought a contemplative smile to Raine's face. Maeva found her manner most intriguing. Raine was in no way reserved and freely displayed a wide range of emotions. But right now, there seemed to be some enormously deep emotion surfacing, an almost melancholy that was completely foreign to the light-hearted warrior.

"Would you like to meet her?" Maeva proffered, surprising even herself.

"I would like that very much," Raine said.

"Then perhaps you would join us on the terrace for morning's meal," Maeva said.

"Thank you," Raine said simply, "I will join you."

There was a lull in the conversation as all sought to process the strange exchange, for even the Ha'kan were aware of the underlying, inexplicable emotion in the conversation. It was Faelon who broke the silence, and did so in a jarring, abrasive manner.

"You're half-Scinterian, are you not?"

Raine pulled herself from her reverie. "There are no half-Scinterians. Either you're Scinterian or you're not."

"That seems a bit of a technicality."

The elf's words were sarcastic, challenging even, and Raine's eye color transitioned back to the ice blue color of her father's people. She held her hands out, palms up, revealing her forearms.

"If you had these burned into your skin as a child," she said, "you would understand it most assuredly is not."

The intricate blue and gold markings rose to the surface, traveling up her arms and over her shoulders, and although unseen, down her back as well. The sight of the ancient filigree was daunting, inspiring fear in the wise and belligerence in the foolish.

"Why do you hide them?" Faelon asked belligerently. "Are you ashamed of them?"

Maeva was not certain why her chief of security was acting like an ass, and she was very near to chastising him publicly, something that was never done by the Alfar when outsiders were present. But Raine had things well in hand.

"I'm very proud of my Scinterian heritage," she said in even tones, "I don't hide them from shame but for the benefit of others."

"How is that?" Faelon asked.

Raine turned her forearms, examining the beautiful scars. "When I was younger, I couldn't control the display of my markings and they were always visible. I was challenged by every insecure fool who thought to prove himself." At this last, her eyes came up to Faelon's, and although the implication was clear, he seemed incapable of stopping himself.

"So, you got tired of fighting."

"No," Raine explained patiently. "I live to fight. And I never get tired of it. And there are many good reasons to kill people. I just didn't think stupidity was one of them."

The utter lethality of the individual in front of him was finally sinking in to Faelon, but just to make certain, Raine finished the conversation.

"I don't hide my markings to protect myself. I hide my markings to protect others from me."

"Faelon, shut up before she kills you," Maeva said crossly. It was unheard of for her to have to speak so in public, and she would have him beaten for this impropriety and breach of protocol.

"I wouldn't kill him without your permission, Ambassador," Raine said politely.

The group quieted and it seemed the tension of the conversation would dissipate when Edwenil determined to escalate it in a completely different manner.

"So, you're Arlanian. Or at least half-Arlanian."

Raine was patient with the invasive question. "Again, there are no degrees. You're either Arlanian or you're not. And yes, I'm Arlanian."

"Show us your eyes."

Maeva was nearly jolted from her chair, having no concept of when she had lost complete control of her staff. Edwenil might as well have asked Raine to disrobe.

The High Priestess immediately assumed her role. "Raine," Astrid said gently, "you don't—"

"It's all right, High Priestess. I'm not ashamed of my mother's people, either."

And as she said this, she looked directly at Astrid, took her by the hand, and revealed her eyes. The Queen's hand fluttered to her breast as the High Priestess caught her breath.

"By the gods," Astrid murmured in appreciation. "Were that your lover more adventurous, or that the Ha'kan had met you before you met her."

"Well," Raine said, her brilliant smile merely highlighting the deep violet of her eyes. "Talan's fortune was to meet the Ha'kan before she met me. I assure you, based on the fondness of her memories, if my love ever feels adventurous, the Ha'kan will be the first to know."

Raine turned her gaze upon Edwenil. "Again, I'm not a typical Arlanian. I'm not helpless or in danger of being enslaved. So, I don't hide my eyes for my sake, but for the sake of others, to save them from the discomfort of my presence."

Maeva fully understood how the Arlanians had been raped into extinction. The Alfar possessed more self-control than any other race, and the lust that Raine inspired in her was staggering. Were Raine less capable of protecting herself, it was possible Maeva would have engaged the military might of the Alfar just to possess her. Of course, there would be that dragon to deal with.

"Come here, lovergirl," Idonea said, draping herself about Raine and pressing her full breasts against the muscled arm. All eyes went to the flesh and the impending exposure that seemed inevitable. Raine grinned as Idonea breathed warmly into her ear.

"My mother sent me down here to rescue you," she whispered, "and if I don't do so quickly, she'll come down and eat the lot of them."

Raine offered Idonea her arm, a gallant gesture that was largely unneeded as she was already wearing Idonea like a cloak.

"I'm going to show my 'daughter' about the room," Raine said with a slight bow. "If you'll excuse me, your Majesty?"

"Enjoy yourself, Raine," Halla said, grateful that Idonea had provided Raine's escape.

And the two moved through the crowd, the center of attention in every group. It was Idonea's habit to flirt outrageously with Raine in social situations, not because it had any effect on Raine, but because it was sheer torture for those around them. And Talan, who did not care to socialize with most mortals, approved because it kept all others at bay. Lorifal, who was used to it, always found it funny.

Maeva watched the pair, one angelically beautiful, the other darkly ravishing, and spoke her thoughts aloud.

"Do you think she sleeps with both the mother and the daughter?"

Anyone else might have been offended by the blunt musing, but to these hosts, it was merely an academic question.

"If Raine were Ha'kan," the Queen said, "that would doubtless be the case. But I think not."

And Maeva smiled, liking the Ha'kan even more.

Raine put her arm about Idonea's waist, who was pressed against her so tightly they seemed fused together, and Raine had shifted to wearing Idonea more as pendant than a cloak. Astrid, although enjoying the show as much as anyone, saw through the ruse with the insight of a High Priestess.

She thought Idonea would have made a very good Priestess, although, she admitted, controlling her would have been impossible.

Raine rejoined Senta, who had since been joined by Gimle.

"You looked like you were having fun over there. I saw you reveal your markings."

"Yes," Raine said, "and my eyes."

"I was certain they were going to ask her to remove her clothes next," Idonea said, laughing.

"I'm more comfortable doing that than showing my eyes," Raine said, also laughing.

Maeva's gaze was still on Raine when musical laughter drifted her way from the group containing the Princess and the dwarves. The little hazel-eyed beauty was telling a story with great animation and the dwarves were enthralled.

"So, that little imp," Maeva said, "she's really the ruler of the Tavinter?"

"Yes," Queen Halla said, "although don't let Skye's youth or appearance mislead you. She waged a guerilla war against the Ha'kan for three years despite scarce resources and a skeletal fighting force."

"And how did this come about?" Maeva asked. This story was of interest for many reasons, not least among them the fact it had re-aligned the geopolitical structure of a large swath of Arianthem.

"Some years ago, Kolgrim, Skye's father, and I began discussing the possibility of a novel experiment. It had been proposed by Isleif, so we gave it great consideration."

"And what was this experiment?" Maeva asked.

"Skye was to attend the Sjöfn Academy and be personally mentored by my daughter, Dallan."

"And we all saw how that turned out," Astrid murmured.

Halla hid a smile. Dallan had violated one of the few, hard, fast edicts for the Ha'kan, which was no sexual activity prior to the Age of Consent. This edict was put in place so that a young woman's sexual awakening could be supervised and made as perfect as possible since sexual enjoyment and skill was so integral to their culture. Dallan had not missed it by much, but she had missed it.

"We had been misled regarding the normal appearance of the Tavinter, thinking them all to be hideously ugly. I believe this began during my grandmother's reign, because she would raid the surrounding lands for beautiful women. This practice fell out of favor with my mother and was abolished by the time I took the throne. But the Tavinter's defense remained in place, the tales of their ugliness spread, and the fable remained for several generations. So, imagine our surprise when that," Halla said, nodding at the girl across the room, "showed up on our doorstep."

"And the Ha'kan welcomed this little Tavinter with open arms, so to speak," Maeva said.

"So to speak," Halla said. "And Skye was eagerly embraced by the Ha'kan in all ways, and we began to appreciate the skills of her people."

"But then Kolgrim was assassinated," Maeva said. The Alfar intelligence network was considerable, and Maeva had tracked these events from a distance.

"Yes," the Queen said, and her expression saddened. "Skye's father was assassinated, and it was made to look as if a rogue unit within the Ha'kan had done such a deed. Then a Ha'kan nursery in Gudrid was destroyed, all the little ones killed, and it was made to look as if the Tavinter had done it in retaliation. And Skye slipped away to take her father's place."

"And the Tavinter and Ha'kan went to war."

"Yes. For three years we fought with the Garmlain to defeat the Tavinter. And for three years Skye held us at bay. We took much of the Tavinter land, but the Tavinter themselves were like ghosts, rarely captured and almost always rescued by their comrades if they were taken."

"But it was the Garmlain who orchestrated this war, correct?" Maeva asked.

"Yes," Halla said, "a fact we realized once we captured Skye, who had given herself up to save her people."

Maeva looked at the young woman across the room with new eyes. It hardly seemed possible that the youngster who blushed so freely and laughed so effortlessly could be such a force to be reckoned with. "And then the Ha'kan turned about and crushed the Garmlain."

"Yes," Halla said, a note of steely satisfaction in her voice, "they were annihilated."

Maeva took notice of this subtle shift, for it seemed the gentle, gracious Ha'kan Queen had a bit of her grandmother in her.

"And so," Maeva said carefully, arriving at the part of the story she had been getting to all along, "the Ha'kan obtained all of Garmlain territory."

"Yes," Halla replied, knowing Maeva's destination from the beginning of the conversation, "the Ha'kan returned all Tavinter land and acquired all Garmlain territory to the border of the Empire. We would not have sought this land through aggression, but we did take it as compensation."

And now Maeva thought that the Ha'kan Queen had more than a little of her grandmother in her. From what her intelligence sources said, the Garmlain fell before the Ha'kan like wheat before a scythe.

"And so," Maeva said, "the Ha'kan gained the most valuable trade routes in all of Arianthem."

"We did," the Queen said, "for these routes offer easy passage to every hold, country, and dominion in the land."

"The Garmlain were possessive with these routes, charging huge sums of money to travel by them."

"No," Halla corrected, "the Garmlain were greedy and they extorted money from vendors, forcing them to pay or travel by more dangerous routes. The Ha'kan have abolished the tolls on the roads."

Maeva could not believe what she was hearing. "And so, you don't charge for passage?"

"No," Halla said, "all who are allies and friends of the Ha'kan are free to travel the routes."

Maeva was stunned, for the Queen was casually conceding all that she had sought to obtain from their meeting. She thought it would take hours of negotiation and skilled diplomacy, and many concessions, and yet the Queen was handing it to her. Still, she had to make certain.

"And the Ha'kan would consider the Alfar in such light?"

"Of course," the Queen said, and then got to the crux of the matter. "The Ha'kan are much like the Alfar in that we're very self-sufficient and need little from anyone else. I dare say we're completely self-contained and need nothing. We, like the Alfar, possess extraordinary military might. But," Halla said, and she was deadly serious, "the threat of the Hyr'rok'kin is such that no one can stand alone."

Maeva slowly nodded. "My brother agrees with you. I, too, would have the Alfar keep to themselves, but he feels this is no longer an option."

"And the Empire has the misfortune of bordering the Empty Land."

The Empty Land was a desert that was nearly impassible, filled with dangerous creatures, no water, and no resources; it had been successfully traversed by only a handful of people. What was on the other side of the Empty Land was even worse, the Veil, a valley that fluctuated between the mortal world and the Underworld, the habitat of demonic monstrosities. And what was on the other side of the Veil was the Gate to the Underworld itself, where Hyr'rok'kin had spewed out spasmodically over the last two decades, spasms which were increasing in size and intensity.

"As much as it might pain you to embrace the idea," Halla said quietly, "both the Ha'kan and the Alfar may have to fight for the Empire and on imperial soil. Otherwise, if the Empire falls, it will become the Empty Land, a desert which will border both our nations."

And Maeva knew she was right. The Empire was vast, the Alfar to its north in the mountains, the Ha'kan to the east in what had previously been Garmlain territory. The dwarves were spread throughout the mountains and deep into the earth north of Garmlain territory, and the Tavinter in the forests and mountains to the north of the Ha'kan. But the Empire's entire western flank was the Empty Land, in quieter times a blessing as it was uninhabited, but now a grave threat as it was the highway for the Hyr'rok'kin.

"It seems your chief supporter among the Alfar has arrived."

A tall, slender, light-haired elf stood in the doorway. He was dressed far simpler than Maeva, his clothing more utilitarian and closer to that of the wood elves than the Alfar. But he so resembled his twin sister there was no hiding his identity.

"Feyden!" Raine exclaimed. She, too, had noted his arrival and approached to greet him. She did so respectfully, with great affection, but did not violate the unwritten social rules of the Alfar. She placed her hands on his shoulders, at arm's length, just drinking in the sight of her friend.

Feyden would have none of that and violated the rules himself. He pulled Raine close and hugged her tightly. He then slapped Lorifal on the back, who had come up as well, and there ensued a great deal of slapping back-and-forth as well as several fully thrown punches between the two. That settled and Idonea approached, and Feyden pulled her close and kissed the cheek she proffered.

Edwenil and Faelon sat with their mouths gaping, for Feyden was usually as reserved as his sister, if not more so. Maeva let loose a great sigh, watching the scene with marked disapproval.

"I imagine a good deal of camaraderie develops between friends who've been through so much," Astrid suggested tactfully.

"Yes," Maeva agreed while her tone did not.

Feyden saw his sister's expression and leaned toward Raine. "If I don't get over there and greet her properly, I will never hear the end of it."

"I just recently made my own escape, but I'll accompany you back over there," Raine whispered back to him.

"You always have my back," Feyden said with a grin.

Feyden approached Maeva, his elder by only minutes but still his elder, and bowed deeply before her.

"Ambassador," he said formally, "forgive the lateness of my arrival."

"Brother," she said drily, but the informal title told Feyden she was not genuinely angry with him. It also gave him leave for a more informal greeting, and he leaned forward and gave her the lightest peck on the cheek she offered him. He stepped back. "Faelon," he said, nodding to the chief of security, "Edwenil."

"No kiss for me?" Edwenil said. Her tone was sarcastic, perhaps a slight condemnation of Feyden's perceived lack of decorum. But there was a little something else in it, the faintest suggestion she would welcome a kiss.

Raine rescued her companion. "Feyden, this is Queen Halla."

Now Feyden was truly flustered, although it hardly showed. He should have greeted the Queen before anyone. He bowed deeply. "I beg your forgiveness, your Majesty. I'm unused to royalty socializing in such informal circumstances."

"It's no matter, Feyden," Halla said, "there's very little ceremony required in a Ha'kan gathering such as this. The informality is purposeful and expected."

"And, Feyden," Raine said, continuing her introductions, "this is Astrid, the High Priestess of the Ha'kan."

Feyden took the hand Astrid extended and brushed his lips across the back of it in a gallant manner that made Maeva wonder when her brother had become such a courtier. "The legend of the beauty of the Ha'kan has fallen far short of the reality."

"Thank you, Feyden," Astrid said, "and welcome to Haldis."

"The Ha'kan have graciously provided us with numerous suites in the guest wing," Maeva said, "although I'm certain you'll be spending most of your time just outside the palace gates."

Feyden looked askance at Raine. "That's where the Dwarven embassy is," Raine explained, "and Lorifal has already laid claim to most of your time."

Maeva made another rude noise giving her opinion on that matter, and Raine again rescued her friend. "Come, Feyden, let me introduce you to the rest of the group."

And so Feyden met all in the room, greeted respectfully by his own kind, with curiosity and enthusiasm by the Ha'kan, and raucously by the dwarves. And although Maeva observed with an outward display of mild disapproval, inwardly she had to admit that Feyden was a favorable counterbalance to her personality when in mixed company.

It was getting later in the evening when Idonea leaned over to Feyden. "She's getting that look on her face again."

Feyden nodded sagely. "She certainly is."

"What look is that?" Raine asked.

"The look you wore almost the entire time we were on our quest," Feyden said.

"The 'I like to kill Hyr'rok'kin' look?"

"Not exactly," Idonea said, "although they're rather close. It's the look you have when you miss my mother."

"Ah," Raine said, "that look is ever-present if my love is not. I just hide it well."

"You're not hiding it at all right now," Feyden said, "so why don't you let me create a little distraction and you can slip away?"

Raine's gratitude was immense. "You always have my back, friend."

True to his word, Feyden attracted all eyes by engaging Lorifal in a spirited competition involving some sort of combination of alcohol, daggers, and juggling. Maeva watched the display with a jaundiced eye, noting that once it was over, the Arlanian had disappeared. The Queen and High Priestess also noted Raine's absence and smiled to one another.

Raine pushed through the double doors into the guest chambers in the Queen's forum. Weynild was waiting for her there and Raine pressed her entire body against her as Weynild wrapped her long arms about her, holding her tightly.

"That was a chore," Raine said, "although the Ha'kan are so gracious they make everything easier."

"I'd hoped that would be the case," Weynild said, burying her face in Raine's hair.

"You are wise, as always. These talks would have gone very differently had they been held in imperial or Alfar territory. I was eavesdropping a bit, but I think the Ha'kan and Alfar have already come to some sort of informal agreement."

Weynild said nothing but held Raine tightly. She leaned back to look at her lover who was deep in thought.

"Was it hard to reveal yourself?"

Weynild felt Raine tense. She could read her lover so well.

"Of course not," Raine said, knowing exactly what Weynild was talking about, "I'm not ashamed of my mother's people."

Weynild took Raine's chin in her hand and gently guided her gaze upward, staring into the violet eyes. "I meant, was it hard to reveal yourself so soon after Hel's touch?"

A muscle in Raine's cheek was prominent as she clenched her jaw. Hel had kissed her and Raine had unwillingly responded, unable to resist the Goddess. Hel brought out the violet in her eyes almost as effortlessly as her love did, and it was a terrible thing for Raine. "Yes," she admitted, "it was hard. It makes me feel vulnerable to do so around anyone but you."

"Well, I for one don't think you should do it around anyone but me." Weynild's voice had the low, throaty, playful tone reserved solely for her, and as always it filled Raine with warmth. Weynild took her hand. "Come," she commanded.

Raine followed her, assuming they were going to bed, but instead Weynild led her to the stained-glass doors.

"And what's this?" Raine asked. "In the mood for a little exhibitionism?"

"You think of only one thing around me," Weynild said.

"That's not true," Raine began, "okay, that is true. But tell me your mind is not always on the same thing."

"Of course, it is," Weynild said, "but come along now."

It had been a wonderful and productive evening, but Maeva was grateful to retire to the guest wing. She looked forward to seeing her young companion, and although she might make excuses to Raine, she made none to herself. She had kept Kiren from the gathering out of jealousy. The young woman had been so sheltered growing up, she did not want to suddenly expose her to a foreign culture, especially when that culture consisted entirely of gorgeous, highly sexual, non-monogamous women.

But she did not see the little beauty in her suite.

"Where is Kiren?" she asked the chief escort of her guards.

"She's out on the terrace star-gazing."

"By herself?"

"Of course not," the guard replied, "she's with a full complement of guards."

Maeva pushed through the stained-glass doors, admiring the scene depicted on the glass and the artistry with which it was rendered. It was dark on the terrace, and Maeva assumed Kiren had requested the torches extinguished so she could better see the stars. She saw the slender figure, flanked by four elven soldiers, and all five seemed frozen in place, their backs to her. She approached quietly as not to disturb them, and joined Kiren's side. When Kiren did not acknowledge her presence, she looked down at the little beauty, who gazed forward into the darkness a look of wonder on her face. Maeva glanced to the guards, who also stared into the blackness in front of them, pure astonishment on their elven features. Maeva looked into the darkness, unable to see what held them all enraptured, when the darkness very subtly shifted in front of them. When it shifted, there was the faintest of scraping, like the sound of rock or shale rubbing against another rock.

Maeva looked up. It wasn't the sound of rock-on-rock. It was the sound of scales moving against tile. And the darkness wasn't moving, the dragon lying on the terrace was, it was just so enormous it could not be seen that close in the blackness. As Maeva's eyes adjusted, she began to make out the dragon's form and realized it was just half of the dragon draped onto the guest terrace while the front half was lying on the Queen's veranda.

"Isn't it beautiful?" Kiren whispered. "Look there," she said, pointing.

The dragon's neck was curled in a serpentine fashion, the great head resting next to the body. And lying on the neck, cradled like a child between two rows of vicious looking spikes, was Raine. She lie draped carelessly over the neck, her face pressed against the warm, reptilian skin beneath the dragon plate, one arm dangling down to where it rested upon the dragon's bony forehead ridge, a leg wrapped about a spinal barb. She was sound asleep.

And Maeva understood something she had previously failed to grasp, something almost everyone failed to grasp. Raine did not simply love the woman who transformed into a dragon; she loved the dragon.

As if sensing this epiphany, one great gold eye opened, the slit pupil staring directly at the startled party of elves. The eye examined them, flicked from one to the other, then dismissed them all by closing once more. The dragon turned its head away, disinterested, and with a gentle exhale of hot air from its nostrils, went back to sleep. Raine did not even stir, except to wrap her arm about a bony protrusion as the dragon adjusted position.

Maeva touched Kiren lightly on the shoulder. "Let's go inside," she said softly, oddly moved by what she had just witnessed. "Best not to awaken a sleeping dragon."

Chapter 5

Raine stretched in the warm light pouring through the stained glass. Stretched, then yawned, then thought about going back to sleep. She chided herself and sat upright. Weynild had left before dawn and here she was lazing about. She got up, splashed some water on her face, ran her fingers through her hair, then threw on a pair of breeches and a cotton shirt. She went out onto the terrace, hoping she had not missed morning meal with Maeva and Kiren. She crossed over the arched passageway to the adjacent verandah. Fortunately, the Ambassador and her companion were getting a late start as well and were just sitting down to a well-laden table.

"Good morning, Ambassador," Raine said.

"Good morning, Raine," Maeva said, "please join us. Kiren, this is a great friend and ally of the Alfar."

Kiren's sapphire eyes glowed with excitement. "You were sleeping with that dragon last night."

Raine smiled her brilliant smile and took the girl's extended hand. "Yes," she said, "that's my love, Talan'alaith'illaria."

"Queen of all Dragons," Kiren translated breathlessly. "I've read your poem a hundred times, 'The Dragon's Lover.'"

"I don't think of that as my poem," Raine said. "And in fact, if Dagna comes with the imperials, you'll get to meet the author."

"How wonderful!" Kiren exclaimed. "This is all so exciting."

Maeva watched the interaction closely, a spark of jealousy threatening to ignite beneath a bare covering of ashes. She wasn't certain, however, which of the participants she was jealous of: Raine or Kiren. And nothing in their interaction was validating that jealousy or fanning the fire in any way, so the ember was slowly dying out. In fact, although there was extreme warmth between the two, there did not seem to be the colossal heat that Raine inspired in everyone. She watched her young lover closely, and although Kiren displayed curiosity and admiration for Raine, she did not display any of the uncontrolled lust that all felt in the presence of the Arlanian. Maeva inwardly breathed a sigh of relief.

"And how do you like Haldis thus far?" Raine asked.

"It's beautiful," Kiren said, "I read about it many times, but I didn't think I would ever get to see it."

Raine glanced to Maeva to include her in the conversation. "I understand you two will get a tour this morning. You'll enjoy that. The gardens are one of the great wonders of Arianthem. The baths," Raine paused, "well I can't even describe them. They're astonishing in their beauty."

"I read about the baths!" Kiren said.

"We will not be going to the baths," Maeva interjected, causing Kiren to giggle. Raine winked at her.

"I got banned from those, too."

Maeva was fairly amazed at the conversation. She could barely be around Raine without fantasizing about all the things she would do to her, and yet her little beauty sat here unfazed, other than a moderate amount of hero-worship which was entirely appropriate. She relaxed, realizing how much she had feared losing the girl to the Arlanian.

"You should definitely ask to see the nurseries. It gives great insight into the Ha'kan as a people and why they are the way they are."

"I understand they're all kept together, almost from birth."

"That's right," Raine said, "from infancy they live together. They're never alone."

"That must be wonderful," Kiren said, and Raine heard a hint of melancholy.

"Do you have any brothers or sisters?" she asked gently.

"No," Kiren said, shaking her head, "I was an only child. I had only my mother and father, and we never left our estate."

Raine had a very good idea why that was so. "Tell me about your parents," she prompted, still gentle.

"My mother was beautiful, very smart, very strong. She was a soldier at one time, but had a good head for business, so when she left the military, she took over running the estate."

"And your father?"

"Incredibly handsome," Kiren said, "but no head for business. He was a wonderful musician and a great artist, and he was the one who taught me to read and encouraged my studies. My mother loved him more than life itself. When he got sick..." Kiren's voice trailed off and her brow furrowed. "She got sick, too. I think she wanted to stay and take care of me, but she couldn't live without him."

Raine felt a lump in her throat. "Let me guess, you look like your father."

"Right," Kiren said brightly, as if the tragedy of her own story had been so absorbed it no longer affected her. "I look almost exactly like him."

Silence settled on the trio and Raine took a drink of the hot tea provided her. It was hard to swallow, but the warmth seemed to soothe the ache in her throat. Maeva also sipped tea while Kiren happily munched on a piece of buttered bread. She swallowed the bread, then dabbed at her mouth with a linen napkin.

"Can I ask a favor of you?"

"Of course," Raine said, setting her cup down.

"Can I see your eyes?"

Maeva started, but Raine did not tense as she had the night before.

"Of course," she said, and allowed her eyes to revert to their natural, violet color.

The surge of lust returned for Maeva and the jealousy with its imprecise target flared. But although Kiren gasped, it was with innocent joy, not desire.

"They're beautiful!" she exclaimed.

And Raine's heart wrenched, for Kiren looked at her as no other had since her mother. The passion between Arlanians was unmatched between chosen pairs, but they were not subject to the uncontrolled lust for one another that all other races experienced. And Kiren looked at her purely, as none other had in three hundred years.

"Your tears are purple, too," Kiren said softly.

And Maeva stared in wonder, for a single tear ran down Raine's cheek like an amethyst-stained raindrop.

"Yes," Raine said simply, "they're purple, too."

The sound of leathery wings dispelled the mood, as if the wind they created stirred and then dissipated the heavy clouds that had settled upon Raine. She brushed the tear from her cheek, and the brilliant smile returned, albeit with the slightest trace of melancholy.

"My love has returned," Raine said, standing up. "Thank you," she said simply, first to Kiren, then to Maeva, and Maeva had the impression she was being thanked for far more than she understood. Raine nodded to the elven guards and made her way across the bridge. A brilliant flash of light blinded the observers from the guest terrace, and then a tall, regal, silver-haired woman stood where the dragon had been. Raine approached and the woman embraced and kissed her. The two briefly talked, and although their conversation could not be heard, it seemed as if the dragon were comforting

Raine because she embraced her once more when they were finished. She then simply held her for a long time, her face buried in Raine's hair.

"That dragon really loves her," Kiren mused, enchanted by the scene.

"Yes," Maeva agreed, "she certainly does."

Raine finished her morning's repast with Weynild in their room. Weynild confessed to having consumed three elk and a bear while flying about, so she merely sipped tea while Raine ate.

"I'm supposed to join a hunting party this afternoon," Raine said, "I hope you left something in the forest for us."

"I was hungry," Weynild said unapologetically. "And I suggest you hunt deer. The venison was excellent, but the bear is still a bit fatty from winter."

"I'll pass along your advice. This is supposed to be a bonding venture, of sorts. Anyone who wants to hunt can join us."

"Did Senta say where you'd be going?"

"Yes," Raine replied, "the forests to the east are filled with game this time of year."

"Hmm," Weynild said, "I wish I had known. I flew to the west this morning. I would have liked to clear your way."

"'Tis no matter," Raine said, unconcerned. "I'll have Skye with me and a few of the Tavinter, so one of us will sense Hyr'rok'kin if they're near."

Weynild leaned over and kissed her. "You just want to kill them all yourself."

"That's true. You know me too well."

Talk of death and destruction always aroused the dragon, so Raine thought a return trip to the bed was imminent, when a knock on the door interrupted.

"Come," Weynild commanded, her disappointment evident.

A member of the Royal Guard entered. "I beg your pardon," she said with deference. "But there's an imperial noblewoman in the palace courtyard, and she has specifically asked to see you, Raine."

"An imperial noblewoman?" Raine said. "That's odd. The imperials aren't expected for another few days."

"Yes, but she's insistent, and she wishes to speak only to you."

"Another paramour?" Weynild said drily.

"Yes, my love," Raine, said, her tone just as mocking. "You know I have so many." She addressed the guard. "Tell her I'll be down in a moment."

The guard left and Weynild rose and started toward the stained-glass doors.

"Where are you going?" Raine asked.

"I thought I might fly out to the east."

"You're not going to leave me even one, are you?"

"Maybe one," Weynild said, pushing through doors. "No more."

Senta stood in the shadowed alcove watching the pair. She had been notified of their arrival and wanted to assess them for any potential threat. They were an interesting couple. The first was a noblewoman, lovely, elegant, dressed in finery that offset a stunning pair of blue-green eyes. At least superficially, she was what she seemed: a wealthy imperial of high title.

The second was the one who caught Senta's eye. This one was trouble. Her clothing was just as well-made, but she was dressed simpler than the noblewoman: a pair of breeches, a silk shirt, and a vest. Her shoulder-length hair was a bit tousled, giving her a rakish look as if she were perennially just climbing out of bed. She had a way of looking about, a certain conservation of movement, a studied wariness that bespoke one constantly playing a role. It was like watching a play in which the actor was so good one might mistake it for real. Senta's eyes narrowed. She wasn't making that mistake. This one was a rogue and a thief. She might have taken them both into custody had they not asked for Raine by name.

"Jorden!" Raine exclaimed as she came down the stairs. "Syn!"

Senta relaxed a little. Now she watched with more curiosity than concern.

Raine clasped both Jorden's hands in her own, and Jorden leaned forward and kissed her lightly on the cheek. She turned to Syn and took her by the arm.

"And look at you, all domesticated."

Syn rolled her eyes. "Hardly. But I'm trying."

"It's a work in progress," Jorden said drolly, "but the lessons are fun."

Now Senta was even more interested, for there was an edge in the noblewoman's voice that indicated she might be more than she seemed. There was an unexpected strength and cunning there, and an overt sexuality that sharpened the exchange. It was evident who was earth and who was sky in that relationship, she thought wryly.

Then, the play took an unexpected twist as Skye came down the stairs, followed by Dallan and Rika. And all three girls recognized the pair as well.

"Syn!" Skye exclaimed, and ran to the lanky figure. And Senta watched as the Ha'kan Princess and future First General also greeted the rogue joyfully, as if they were long-time friends.

Syn accepted Skye's embrace, then stepped back a little uncomfortably. "Shouldn't I bow to you or something?" she said with a trace of accusation. "You could have told me who you were."

"It didn't seem that important at the time," Skye said cheerfully.

"And you," Syn said, turning to Dallan, "are royalty. By the gods, you could have said something."

"Like Skye said," Dallan repeated, "it didn't seem that important at the time." She turned and bowed to the noblewoman. "And I welcome the Lady Jorden to the Ha'kan palace."

"Thank you, your Highness. And may I say, you three are better dressed than the last time I saw you," Jorden said, "in that tavern in Trygg."

That was definitely true as the three had traveled inconspicuously, hooded and cloaked most of the journey. Now Dallan wore royal vestments, Rika wore her gleaming armor, and Skye was dressed in the garments of Tavinter rulers. Syn sighed out loud. She was out-of-place before, now she was completely in over her head.

"But I didn't think you were coming," Raine said, addressing Jorden. "I'd hoped for your insight on a number of matters, not to mention the fact you're one of the few imperials that Maeva actually likes."

"It's that 'insight' that's brought me here," Jorden said, growing serious. "And I need to speak with you privately." Her blue-green eyes flicked to the shadowed alcove. "And if that very large woman glowering at us from the corner is the Ha'kan First General, as I suspect, she needs to be in on the conversation as well."

Sensing her cue, Senta left the alcove and approached. Raine clasped her arm.

"Senta, this is the Lady Jorden, a trusted friend of mine."

This was all the validation that Senta required, and she bowed respectfully.

"Welcome to Haldis, my lady," she said formally.

"Thank you, First General." Jorden turned to Syn. "My love, why don't you go play with your friends for a while. I know you don't care for business."

To a less keen eye, the exchange would have appeared insulting, even denigrating. But to Senta's practiced eye, she saw the game that was played by these two, the constant interplay of dominance and submission. Syn gave the

Lady Jorden a sardonic look and the Lady Jorden responded with a searing glance that effectively communicated the former would probably spend the evening tied spread-eagle to the bedposts.

"Let's go to my chambers," Raine suggested, and Jorden followed her lead. Rika and Dallan grabbed Syn by the arm.

"Let's head out to the courtyard where we can catch up," Dallan said, and Skye made as if to fall in behind them.

"Skye."

Skye stopped abruptly at Senta's command. She watched with envy as Dallan and Rika made a quick escape. Dallan glanced back over her shoulder apologetically, and Skye couldn't help but notice she didn't even slow down. When she turned, only Senta stood there.

"Yes, First General?"

Senta tried to maintain her stern façade, but it was so difficult with Skye. The Tavinter could not lie to save their lives, and Skye was the most transparent of all of them.

"Do you have plans this evening?"

"What?" Skye said, startled. That was not the question she was anticipating. "Um, no, no, I have no plans."

"I want you in my chambers at 7th bell. Then you can tell me in detail how you know the Lady Jorden and that thief."

Skye hung her head, knowing she was sunk. "Very well, First General."

Senta successfully hid her smile until Skye had scurried from the room, then headed to the Queen's forum.

"Come," Raine said in response to the light knock on the door, and Senta entered. Jorden had removed her traveling cloak but was still standing. As soon as the door closed, Jorden addressed Raine.

"I've received disturbing news, news I felt you needed to hear firsthand."

"The Lady Jorden," Raine explained to Senta, "has an intelligence network that rivals the Alfar's. Some would argue it's even better."

"Really?" Senta said with a trace of skepticism in her voice. "Not many private individuals could claim such a network."

"Not many private individuals are the head of the Guild of Thieves," Jorden said.

Senta blanched at the simple statement. It was too startling a comment to be untrue, a falsehood so improbable it had the ring of truth.

"You're Lagmann?" Senta said slowly.

"I am," Jorden replied.

The blunt revelation was humorous to Raine, who knew Jorden's secret, but surprising.

"I knew once the Tavinter knew my identity," Jorden explained, "it was a matter of time before it became known. Skye is the worst liar I've ever seen." She gave Senta a once-over that communicated appreciation for her size and shape. "And it's not likely she'll hold out long under the interrogation she's going to get from you later."

Senta's face remained impassive, but she inwardly acknowledged that the Lady Jorden was formidable in a multitude of ways. And she was beginning to like her despite the disrepute of her admitted profession.

"So, what's this news, Jorden?"

"Once the imperials arrive, there will be an assassination attempt."

Both Raine and Senta became deadly serious. "An assassination attempt against whom?" Raine asked.

"That's just it," Jorden said. "I don't know. I don't know the target, and I don't know the assassin. This information was obtained, shall we say, in a deathbed confession. But my sources say it's valid."

"So, everyone will be here," Senta said, "the imperials, the Alfar, and the Dverger, and someone will strike at someone."

"Don't forget the Ha'kan and Tavinter," Jorden said pragmatically, "if you're going to be objective about the threat, you can't leave anyone out."

As much as Senta hated to admit it, Jorden was right. Although she thought it extremely unlikely any within the Ha'kan could be the assassins, her beloved Queen or Princess could be the target. Or Skye. Or some disgruntled Tavinter could try and take them all out.

Raine echoed her thoughts aloud. "There are many long-standing feuds in this gathering of people, animosities that have simmered for centuries."

"And you can't rule out that someone might be trying to frame someone else," Jorden pointed out.

"Right," Raine said, "this is an impossible situation."

"Then perhaps we should cancel the gathering," Senta said, "I won't risk my Queen in this."

"We won't get another opportunity like this," Weynild said, coming through the stained-glass doors. She had not heard the entire conversation, but she had heard enough.

"Talan," Jorden said, curtsying deeply. She had not known the dragon queen before, but she knew her now. Weynild nodded to her, but turned her golden gaze back to Raine, who had locked eyes with her upon her entry.

"You're right," Raine said. "And worse, we can't say anything, for that will sow seeds of distrust and destroy the alliance as sure as an assassin's blade."

"Which might be the purpose in the first place. It might be just as easy to get everyone suspecting everyone else, and all is lost."

Jorden agreed. "It's possible this information was planted. That's always a possibility."

"That would speak to deep manipulation on the part of someone," Weynild mused.

"Just so I'm clear on everything," Senta said, frustrated, "there may or may not be an assassination attempt. We don't know the target or the assassins, and no one but the four of us can know."

"That pretty much sums it up," Raine said, sighing.

"How can you expect me to say nothing?" Senta demanded. "How in the world does this event not happen?"

"Because I won't let it."

The words were steel and struck with the sharpness of that metal. Senta gazed into the ice blue eyes of the last Scinterian, reminded that this was the dragon slayer, the destroyer of worlds, the warrior who had assaulted the gates of the Underworld then closed them through sheer force of will. This was the progeny of a people who breathed fire and bled ice. This was an unstoppable force who laughed at pain, taunted death, and never suffered defeat. And the dragon looked upon her lover with pride, not because of the certainty of her assertion, but because it was most certainly true.

"Then that's enough for me," Senta said quietly. "I'll say nothing, and do anything you ask."

"We'll stop this, my friend," Raine said. "There's no doubt."

Chapter 6

Because Jorden had been specific no attempt would occur before the arrival of the imperials, Senta and Raine thought it safe to continue with plans for the hunt. Still, both had a heightened sense of vigilance they sought to conceal. Senta determined she would stay behind with the Queen and accompany them on the tour. Maeva was pleased to see Jorden, and the noblewoman and her companion joined the tour as well. Feyden and Lorifal were eager to go on the hunt and were accompanied by several from their own entourages. Edwenil, accompanied by Faelon, also joined the excursion and Raine wondered if Edwenil's participation had more to do with Feyden than any desire to hunt, although she proved surprisingly capable in the rustic environment. And of course, Skye, Dallan, and Rika had to follow Raine wherever she went.

So, it was a fair-sized party that left for the eastern woods. A few Ha'kan and Tavinter accompanied Dallan and Skye, rounding out the group. There was an air of festivity, an excitement that was disproportional to an average hunt, and Raine thought it might be the novel make-up of the participants. Never had Arianthem seen such a diverse group of individuals on a simple outing.

And each group watched the other curiously. The dwarves carried weapons so heavy it was doubtful the Tavinter could have lifted them.

The Tavinter moved with such stealth that even the graceful Alfar were impressed. The Alfar were such proficient archers they rivaled the gifted Tavinter. The Ha'kan moved with such military precision the dwarves were in awe. The easy camaraderie between the Ha'kan and Tavinter was evident, and the Alfar took note of this bond, incredulous that it could be so strong so soon after years of acrimony. And the dwarves were delighted with the good-natured teasing that went on between the Ha'kan and their former enemies.

And each began to appreciate the strengths of the other peoples in a way that would have been impossible in a more competitive setting. Raine watched with pleasure as the Tavinter tracked a huge bear, led it into a trap where it was contained by fire from the Alfar archers, then finished off by Lorifal, Rika, and the dwarves.

Feyden observed the kill, silently thanking Skaði, the Goddess of the hunt. This was more of a wood elf custom than Alfar, but it was one he practiced, nonetheless.

"Talan said the venison was better than bear, but that one might be good," Raine commented.

"So she eats in dragon form?" Feyden asked.

"Yes, even in human form she sometimes maintains her dragon appetite. Well, appetites," she corrected, eliciting a sly grin from Feyden. "She was out this morning, said she found a few pockets of Hyr'rok'kin and cleared them out."

"I'm glad to hear you say that," Feyden responded, "I've had the feeling we're being followed."

"We are," Raine said without explanation.

Rika stood over the bear, and Gruna, the only dwarf Rika had confirmed as female, stood near her. "So, how are we going to get this back to the capital?" Gruna asked.

Lorifal frowned. He didn't want to break off from the hunt, nor did any of his people. But it would be a waste to leave the game here.

"We have that covered," Skye said, slinging her bow over her back as she approached. Lorifal appreciated the offer but did not see how the slight-framed people could manage the weight of this monster.

"No insult intended, lass, but there are but a handful of your people here."

Rika shook her head. "The Tavinter never travel as 'a handful,' and they're never very far from their leader."

Skye raised her hand and made several deliberate motions in sign language. To Lorifal's eye, she seemed to be signing to the empty forest, but to his astonishment, the forest surrounding them came to life. Things that looked like trees or bushes or piles of brush, peeled away from their camouflage and revealed themselves to be people. One handsome, grinning young man approached Skye.

"Aeric," Skye said, "could you have this bear skinned and quartered, then carried back to the capital?

"Of course," he said cheerfully. "And that was a marvelous kill. A beautifully coordinated trap."

This was a significant complement from a Tavinter scout, and Skye clapped him on the shoulder.

"Thank you, my friend."

"By the gods," Feyden muttered under his breath, "they're like ghosts."

"There's a reason why the Tavinter held off the Ha'kan for so many years," Raine said quietly in agreement.

Feyden was not the only Alfar duly impressed by the display of stealth. The Alfar were astonished they had been unknowingly surrounded. Faelon took careful note of this ability, appeasing himself with the thought that at least the Tavinter, as a people, were few in number. But he began to understand the symbiotic relationship between the Ha'kan and Tavinter, and to understand how potentially dangerous that alliance could prove. The Ha'kan with their numbers, military might and brilliant strategy, and the Tavinter with their stealth and guerilla style, would be a forbidding combination.

The dwarves were nothing but pleased by the feat, appreciating it as one would a magic trick. Gruna banged on her shield with enthusiasm, the traditional dwarven salute.

Feyden noticed that Raine was doing very little other than coordinating movement. He was disappointed. He had looked forward to her displaying her astonishing skills for his people, but she seemed to be deliberately downplaying her abilities. It made him curious, and a little suspicious, because it reminded him of her manner when he had first met her decades before. She had appeared apathetic, lethargic even, and had lulled their party into thinking she was unskilled and cowardly, right up until she had demolished a Marrow Shard without trying. In hindsight, he realized it had been a test, one which they all had failed. It taught him a valuable lesson about judging by appearances, one that he had never forgotten.

Although Raine was neither lethargic nor apathetic now, she was not revealing any of her formidable talents, and it made him wonder why. Perhaps he was overthinking it; perhaps she just wanted the focus to be on the various parties involved in the treaty discussions.

The hunt continued and the participants brought down enough game to provide for several feasts. Although initially each group tended to clump together, soon they were mixing with one another freely. Even Edwenil deigned to speak to the Tavinter when her curiosity outweighed her pride. She had watched them for some time as they casually plucked leaves or roots from the forests around them, tucking them into the leather pouches they all carried on their belts. Aeric explained to her the various herbs and potions that could be ground or mixed from the plants of the forest, and how the Tavinter, because of their nomadic ways, were in a constant state of hunting and gathering. The forest people did not grow crops, rather harvested everything around them. Although the Alfar had alchemists and trades that specialized in such knowledge, their skill paled in comparison to the utilitarian understanding of the Tavinter.

They were about as deep in the forest as they were going to go, Raine flanked on one side by Lorifal and Feyden on the other. The three were content to talk quietly and had moved some ways away from the main group, which had become dispersed. This had put them on the leading edge of everyone, slightly to the south. Even though they were no longer hunting, Raine stepped softly out of habit, and Feyden and Lorifal followed her lead. And when she stopped abruptly, her words cut off into absolute stillness and silence, they also followed suit.

"Skye," Raine said, the word so soft it was barely audible. But Skye materialized at her side.

"What is it?" Skye said, just as softly.

"I'm not sure," Raine whispered. She glanced to Lorifal, who shook his head, and then to Feyden, who did the same. She gazed into the forest in front of them, her senses straining. Skye did the same, her heart pounding in her chest. There was only one thing that Raine was able to sense better than the Tavinter.

"Skye," Raine said, still whispering, "Signal your people to round up the others. Get behind us, we're going to move slowly in that direction. I—," Raine paused, frowning. "I don't know what this is."

This statement made Skye's heart pound even harder, but she disappeared noiselessly into the forest behind them. And within a short span, the group was corralled by grim-faced Tavinter who had transitioned from light-hearted to deadly serious with a single hand signal from their leader.

Dallan and Rika joined Skye, and the three crept back toward Raine, who was moving with great caution. Everyone was moving silently, but Raine debated sending everyone back. By the looks on the faces of those immediately surrounding her, however, she knew that would prove a fruitless task. They pressed forward.

Soon everyone could hear what Raine sensed, but did not recognize it, either. To some it sounded like a low, rhythmic rumble that repeated at regular intervals. To Raine, used to sleeping with a dragon, it sounded like the breathing of a very large creature. She frowned, then signed to Skye. Her plan was to have the group fan out into a half-moon shape, half-surrounding whatever was in front of them, but from a distance. Skye signed to her Tavinter scouts, who maneuvered everyone into position.

It was a dragon. A dragon lying in a small meadow surrounded by trees. It was not as large as Talan, and pure white, although its scales had the same iridescent quality as did Talan's, throwing off tiny rainbows in every direction and giving the dragon's skin a pearl-like finish. The dragon's head rested on its forelegs in a casual pose, and its eyes were bright blue as they looked at Raine, even though she was still within the cover of the forest.

"Well," Raine murmured, "she obviously knows I'm here."

To her companions' shock and dismay, Raine stood upright and left her place of concealment, walking openly into the clearing.

The dragon smiled and raised her head. The great smile was terrifying, revealing endless rows of fangs, but it did not faze Raine, who was more disturbed by what she could not see than what was in front of her.

"You're not a dragon."

"Hmmm...." was all the dragon said, and her voice was indeed female. She seemed to take great pleasure in examining Raine.

Raine cocked her head to the side. She was used to being stared at, but this stare was different. There was no desire or lust in the gaze, which was extraordinary coming from any creature, let alone a dragon.

"Your parents are very proud of you."

Raine frowned. That was a very random statement. "You speak of them in the present when they're both dead. So, perhaps you're not of this world."

The dragon smiled wider. "So close to the truth by completely the wrong path. There are many things here that do not belong in this world."

Raine wasn't sure if she was speaking of "here" as in something near by in the forest, or merely in the larger sense of the Hyr'rok'kin invasion. The dragon did not appear as if she would elaborate and continued to drink in the sight of Raine, as if some long-denied need was being satisfied. Those in the surrounding forest watched, frozen in place, fascinated.

"The matter before you now," the dragon rumbled, "the one brought to you this morning."

Raine grew very still. She knew exactly what the dragon was talking about.

"You must ask yourself but one question."

"Which is?" Raine asked.

"Who else has the most to gain?"

It was the question Raine had been asking herself for hours, albeit peculiarly worded. It would help to know who the target of the assassination was to determine who would have the most to gain. And even then it could be a convoluted affair.

"It will become perfectly clear. That which seems to matter doesn't at all." the dragon said, and then fell into silence. Her deep breathing was the only sound in the meadow. She seemed to contemplate many things, and her expression grew impassive and her tone mildly regretful.

"You have many dark days ahead of you."

Raine's tone was even. "I know that."

"The prophecy will be fulfilled."

"I know," Raine said, then more firmly. "But I'll make my own destiny."

The dragon's eyes narrowed, as if Raine had just suggested a possibility she had not considered, one she need meditate upon and contemplate fully.

"I guess we will see."

The statement had a tone of finality, and upon the last word, the dragon disappeared, leaving behind a rainbow that outlined the shape of the dragon, and then nothing at all. The other members of the hunting party began to slowly exit the surrounding forest as if rousing from a magical spell.

Feyden, who had seen many strange things in his adventures with Raine, thought this was one of the strangest.

"Do you know who or what that was?" he asked.

Raine stared at the empty spot where the dragon had been lying, noting that the grass wasn't even disturbed where the creature had been.

"I don't have the slightest idea."

The hunting party returned to the palace. The hunt had been productive and even better, a resounding success in fostering respect and camaraderie among the participants. But it was the final event of the day that had everyone talking. The sighting of a white dragon that had conversed of peculiar, oblique things with the Scinterian was magical, and really without explanation. Raine spoke little and much to everyone's disappointment, retired to her quarters where Weynild was waiting.

"You've heard?" Raine asked, her expression moody.

"I've heard many fantastic things, but I thought I would get the best account from you."

And so Raine related the encounter in its entirety, trying to remember every last detail and word.

"I don't recognize this creature from your description," Weynild mused, "so I'm inclined to agree it wasn't a dragon. And you believe the matter she spoke of was the assassination?"

"It would seem, although she was deliberately vague."

"She looked at me so strangely," Raine continued, "it kind of reminded me of the way Kiren looked at me this morning."

"How so?"

"Kiren looked upon me as one Arlanian to another, without any lust or avarice, like others."

"Including me," Weynild said drily.

A grin tugged at the corner of Raine's mouth and Weynild was pleased to see Raine's mood lighten a bit. "I'd be troubled if you didn't look at me that way. But it grows tiresome from others."

"Then this creature was definitely not a dragon," Weynild said. There was not one of her kind that could resist the Arlanian Scinterian in front of her.

"No," Raine said, still thinking hard. "No, in fact, out of all of the creatures I've come across in three centuries, I really couldn't place the feel of this one. It was very powerful, but not necessarily with magic...."

Raine's words drifted off.

"What?" Weynild prompted.

"Strangely, I can only compare the sensation to one other being that I've been around."

"And who's that?" Weynild asked, a finger of unease tracing its way up her spine.

"My old friend Fenrir."

CHAPTER 7

Lorifal meandered down the hall, searching for Feyden. Feyden was spending much of his time in the Dwarven embassy but had taken chambers in the palace to satisfy his sister. Lorifal agreed it was easier to accede to Maeva's wishes than defy her openly. The Ha'kan sentries directed him along the twists and turns to the wing where Maeva's staff was quartered. He was just about to enter into the wing when whispered voices caught his attention. His nose twitched, much as it did when he was near a vein of gold, and he backed into a nearby alcove. He was not one to eavesdrop, but nor was he one to ignore instincts that had served the dwarves for millennia.

"And you're sure she still suspects nothing?" a male voice said.

"I'm certain," the female said, "and I flirt with her brother to allay suspicion. No one suspects anything. This plan should work perfectly."

"And you're certain it'll succeed? If we're found out, we'll both face banishment."

"Banishment?" the female voice said sarcastically, "we'll face death. But if we succeed, our future is secured."

The voices grew silent and a rustling of clothing indicated the conspirators were leaving. Lorifal risked a glance around the corner and could see the departing back of the male. He was pretty sure it was Maeva's Chief of

Security, Faelon, or whatever his name was. Lorifal waited a moment, then hurried on to Feyden's room.

"You're certain it was Faelon?" Feyden asked after Lorifal described the encounter.

"I would swear by my ancestors," Lorifal said. "I don't care for that arrogant bastard and would surely recognize him."

"Then my guess is that the female was Edwenil. She 'flirts' with me while they plot against my sister," he said angrily.

"Are you going to tell Maeva?" Lorifal asked.

That was Feyden's first impulse, to run to his sister and tell her. But there were too many important things happening right now. The threat of the Hyr'rok'kin was too great to interrupt the negotiation of alliances.

"No," Feyden said, "I won't let some internal Alfar power struggle derail these talks. No one must know of this plot other than you and me. And we must protect Maeva."

"No one?" Lorifal asked.

"Well, Raine of course," Feyden said, as if that had been a given, "she'll help us protect my sister."

There was no formal gathering that evening, but many from all camps joined in the impromptu buffet in the courtyard. Meat from the hunt had been skillfully prepared by the royal kitchen staff, and food and drink was plentiful. The Queen and her staff made an appearance, as did Maeva and hers, but many retired early, leaving behind the younger and more rambunctious of the groups. Raine did not appear, disappointing many, but the disappointment did not last long as the merriment increased.

Skye disappeared shortly before 7th bell, and Dallan and Rika were surprised to see her reappear in the courtyard a short time later. Both had assumed Skye would spend the night with Senta, as was her custom, but Senta had been pulled away on some matter of which she would say little. In truth, Senta would be sleeping with her Queen until the assassination target was identified. And she had agreed with Raine that Idonea should be added to the inner circle of four who knew of the possible attempt because Idonea was staying in Dallan's forum and could quietly protect both Dallan and Skye.

"So, did you tell on me?" Rika demanded.

"You know I did," Skye said, frowning. "Senta has only to look at me with that stern look and I tell her everything."

"What did she say?"

"She was appalled that you insulted Gruna. But then she admitted it was kind of hard to tell the male and female dwarves apart, so I don't think you're in that much trouble."

"Thank the gods," Rika muttered. "It really wasn't on purpose."

"Did you tell her about Lagmann?" Dallan asked.

"She already knew!" Skye exclaimed. "I had no idea what I was going to say when she asked, but she saved me the trouble. Apparently, Jorden already told her about the Guild of Thieves."

"That's odd," Dallan said. "Is Jorden revealing her alter ego?"

"No, definitely not," Skye said. "Senta was quite clear on that. I'm still to keep the secret. Or at least to the best of my abilities," she added, reddening a little.

"Then why do you think Jorden told Senta?"

"I don't know," Skye said. "And I know Senta is going to spend the night with the Queen, which isn't unusual..."

"But?"

"I got the impression there might have been a reason beyond pleasure."

Dallan grew contemplative. Now that she thought about it, Senta had not left her mother's side since Jorden had arrived. Raine had acted normal all day, but there seemed to be a subtle, heightened awareness about her. And Idonea, who leaned against the wall, laughing with Feyden and Lorifal, watched them with an intentness Dallan at first found flattering, but now thought might have an ulterior motive.

"Something's going on."

Skye nodded. "I agree. But I don't know what. Senta told me the imperials are making surprisingly good time and might be here as early as tomorrow."

"Then we'll all be on our guard," Dallan said firmly, and Rika nodded her agreement.

A troubled look passed over Skye's features.

"What's wrong now?"

"Torsten spoke to me earlier, and I didn't think much about what he said. But now I wonder if it's significant."

"What did he say?"

"Right after the hunt, he was approached by one of our scouts from the Deep Woods. The scout was relaying rumors, nothing more than conjecture."

"What kind of rumors?" Rika asked.

"Rumors of some disgruntled amongst my people. Some who still bear a grudge against the Ha'kan."

"That seems hard to believe," Dallan said, "your people are absolutely loyal to you. Even those who might not care for us won't disobey you."

Skye was grateful for the reassurance. "I can't imagine it myself, but after Gudrid, I won't take any chances."

The mention of Gudrid made all three solemn. Gudrid was a Ha'kan nursery that had been destroyed years before, all the infants and caretakers slaughtered. The act allegedly had been in retaliation for the assassination of Kolgrim, Skye's father, which had allegedly been perpetrated by a rogue unit within the Ha'kan. These two events sparked a three-year war between the Ha'kan and Tavinter, and it wasn't until its end that the two nations learned that both acts had been committed by the Garmlain in order to pit the Ha'kan and Tavinter against one another. The Tavinter had suffered greatly and would have been destroyed without Skye's leadership.

"Gudrid was not destroyed by the Tavinter," Dallan said firmly.

"And my father was not assassinated by the Ha'kan," Skye reminded her, "but there still might be those who lost loved ones in the war and are bitter."

"I worry about that myself," Rika confessed, "as does Senta. It's always a security concern."

"I've sent both Aeric and Flynt to look into the matter. Perhaps you should relay this to Senta?" Skye said, addressing Rika.

Although Skye had the most informal of relationship with the First General, she also respected protocol. It felt more appropriate for this information to be forwarded by Rika as the future First General.

"I'll do so first thing in the morning," Rika agreed.

Chapter 8

It was a far smaller and less organized procession than the Alfar that entered Haldis. In fact, the imperials barreled through the Ha'kan capital on horseback at the same breakneck speed they had conducted their entire journey. Many soldiers wondered what was driving the Knight Commander. Although Nerthus was known to focus on her duties with intensity, none had seen her quite so obsessed with a mission before and quietly commented that the welfare of the heir to the House of Storr must be of great concern to the Emperor.

Raine had convinced the Queen that a much smaller, more informal ceremony was appropriate to greet the arriving imperial cohort, and Senta had strongly backed the suggestion. In fact, Raine proposed that she be the one to greet the few dozen soldiers, accompanied only by representatives from the peoples present. Raine had hand-picked those who would stand with her on the first landing, so Feyden was present for the Alfar, Lorifal present for the dwarves, Skye present for the Tavinter, and of course, Skye could go nowhere without Dallan and Rika, who represented the Ha'kan. The Queen and her staff stood on the upper landing. On the terraces above them, Maeva stood with Edwenil, Faelon, and an excited Kiren, who looked down on the assembly with wide eyes. Some distance away, Idonea stood, and was joined by her mother whose amber eyes took in all below.

Raine started down the steps toward them as the Knight Commander dismounted. There was a second figure dismounting, however, that caught Raine's attention, one of equal rank to Nerthus. This Knight Commander was unexpected but greatly welcome. Raine quickened her step, as did Lorifal and Feyden. The Knight Commander broke into a wide grin at the sight of the three of them, his ruddy complexion bright with exertion and pleasure, his cheeks nearly the color of his red hair.

"Bristol!" Raine exclaimed, and clasped forearms with the imperial officer.

"Raine!" Bristol said, equally excited to see his friend. He turned to Lorifal and Feyden, and much backslapping ensued. His soldiers were surprised at the enthusiastic greeting. They had been briefed to expect a polite but cold welcome, and this was nothing of the sort. And when it did not seem the level of excitement could get any higher, the imperial bard dismounted, followed by a doe-eyed elven mage, and the group erupted into elation.

"Dagna!"

"Elyara!"

And again, much backslapping and hugging ensued, albeit slightly more gentle with Elyara as she was a slender thing. The six formed an impromptu circle, shoulder-to-shoulder, and Raine glanced up at Idonea who smiled down on her companions. Raine placed a hand on Lorifal's and Feyden's shoulders, and then they all did so, forming an unbreakable chain.

"This is an auspicious sign," Raine said, pleased beyond measure. "We're together again."

And although few in the courtyard were aware of the fact, they were in the presence of greatness. For the seven before them had been the intrepid band of adventurers that traveled through the Veil to the Gates of the Underworld twenty years before and stopped the Hyr'rok'kin dead in their tracks. With the help of Talan'alaith'illaria, they had defeated the black dragon and destroyed the great Scales of Light and Dark that held open the doors. And Dagna, who had met Elyara on the quest, immortalized the adventure in the epic poem "The Dragon's Lover."

"Is that—? Are they—?" Dallan whispered. The three stood a respectful distance back.

"It is and they are," Skye whispered back, breathlessly. "That's the band that went to the Underworld two decades ago."

Under normal circumstances, Nerthus would have been angered that she was ignored in the greeting. But she was oblivious to the slight, for no sooner had she dismounted, her eyes began scanning every figure in view until at last they settled on the raven-haired mage standing on the terrace above.

Idonea became aware of the scrutiny and cast an amused, sultry look in her direction. Weynild also became aware of the Knight Commander's pronounced scrutiny, as well as its object.

"Really my dear?" she said drily.

"What?"

"I know you enjoy the company of men, but that is the most manly thing I've seen you with in some time."

"And that was mean even for you, mother," Idonea said, laughing.

"No, no," Kara said, having joined the two on the terrace. She was assessing the Knight Commander in a methodical manner. "Imperial armor is very unflattering, especially for females." She finished her visual appraisal, satisfied with her conclusion. "She has magnificent breasts underneath that armor."

"You have a good eye, First Scholar," Idonea said, and Kara was pleased, not by the compliment or the title, but by the accuracy of her assessment.

Weynild made a rude noise, the equivalent of snorting fire in her dragon form.

Raine extricated herself from the circle and approached Nerthus.

"I beg your forgiveness, Knight Commander," Raine said, "I was excited to see my friends and forgot my manners. Welcome to Haldis." She waved to Dallan and Skye, and they started over.

Nerthus examined the stunning, lethal creature in front of her. The last time she had seen the woman, she had been dismissive of her name when introduced, thinking her a mere mercenary. She had noted with sarcasm that half the people in Arianthem were named "Raine" after Dagna's stupid poem was published.

"You could have told me that you were *the* Raine," Nerthus said gruffly.

Raine flashed her a brilliant smile. "I prefer to let my actions speak for themselves. Knight Commander, this is Dallan," Raine said as the trio approached.

Nerthus took note of the Ha'kan royal insignia and was uncertain of the appropriate greeting. Dallan saved her the trouble and simply extended her hand in the most informal of greetings, warrior to warrior. Nerthus clasped her forearm in surprise.

"You're the Princess?" Nerthus said, stuttering slightly.

"Yes," her Royal Highness, Future Queen of the Ha'kan said, "but please call me Dallan. And this is Rika, my future First General."

Nerthus clasped forearms with the other young woman. Nerthus was large for a female human and enjoyed towering over most others, male and female. But the Princess was her height and the other towered over her. Their manner was so warm and friendly, however, it did not elicit her usual reaction, which was to become threatened and defensive.

Queen Halla watched the exchange from above, delighted with her daughter and Rika. Raine had been exactly right. There would have been all sorts of awkwardness and uncertainty over protocol given imperial unpredictability. With the Alfar and Dverger it was simple and straightforward: ceremony and etiquette ruled all. But the sons and daughters of men could be insulting in their familiarity or embarrassing in their adulation. Raine's approach had removed all of that from the equation.

"And this is Skye," Raine said, continuing the introductions. "She's the ruler of the Tavinter and commander of the Ha'kan Rangers."

Nerthus shook hands with the young woman, again startled. She had heard tales of this one's exploits, but the slender figure in front of her seemed barely old enough to be out of the Academy.

"I'm very pleased to meet you, Knight Commander."

Nerthus was very out of sorts. Although her secret motivation had been to see Idonea, her principle mission was to ascertain the status of the heir to the House of Storr, to ensure that the young woman was not being held captive by the Alfar, and that her health and mental state were good. Nerthus anticipated the affair would be difficult and strained. None of that seemed to be occurring.

"And if you'll look up," Raine said, "you can see the heir to the House of Storr right there."

Nerthus' eyes went magnetically right to Idonea, whose lips twitched into a wicked smile.

"No, no," Raine said, gently redirecting her while Dallan suppressed a grin, "over there."

Nerthus glanced over to a small figure standing next to the elven ambassador. The raven-haired figure waved to Raine with enthusiasm and Raine waved back.

"Well, she looks healthy enough," Nerthus admitted.

"I believe that you and I and the young lady are going to have lunch on the terrace."

Surprisingly, Maeva had been the one to suggest this combination of participants, having calculated it to be the most probable of success and the least probable to create conflict. And for whatever reason, she now trusted the Arlanian with her young lover more than she trusted anyone in Arianthem.

"Perhaps Bristol can come as well," Raine mused, not having anticipated his presence but thinking he would be a good addition. "And I believe you know Idonea, so we should invite her, also."

"That would be acceptable," Nerthus said, trying to appear as if it were no matter, and utterly failing.

"Good," Raine said breezily, "We'll get you and your troops settled, then eat."

Nerthus started down the hallway towards the stairway that led to the terraces. Her men were settled comfortably, their spent horses receiving exceptional care in the Ha'kan stables. Bristol had disappeared with that fair-haired elf and dwarf, saying he would meet her at the appointed time. She had debated removing her armor and wearing something more casual, but she was not that comfortable yet. Perhaps when her formal business was finished.

She had almost reached the stairwell when her forward progress was blocked by a figure stepping from the shadows, one that towered over her even more so than the Ha'kan. The figure was slender, but only because the fiery red armor she wore was so form-fitting it seemed a part of her, the scaled plates moving in perfect coordination, the spikes extending outward in every direction. Her hair was silver, and her gold eyes inspected the Knight Commander with something close to disdain. She was a gorgeous, regal, electrifying creature, and Nerthus, who had faced enemies without fear for decades, felt a primitive terror wrap its icy fingers around her heart.

The woman's amber eyes lowered to a spot in the center of the Knight Commander's breastplate. Very slowly, she raised one arm so covered in spikes it could have been used as a mace. Nerthus did not know her intent but was frozen in place. She did not resist or even move when one long finger hooked beneath the chain she wore and slowly began pulling the necklace from beneath her armor.

The vial came free and dangled between the two of them. The bright red liquid began to softly glow as soon as the woman looked upon it. Her eyes returned to Nerthus and the Knight Commander felt as if she were being peeled layer-by-layer, skin, then flesh, then bone, dissected and examined with a gaze that produced so much heat Nerthus was surprised she did not burst into flames. The gaze assessed, evaluated, judged, and in the end, Nerthus had no idea how she fared or what the verdict had been. But the silver-haired woman slowly tucked the vial back into her armor, patting the top of the breastplate in a condescending gesture. The silver-haired woman then spun about on her heel and was gone as quickly as she had appeared.

Nerthus swallowed hard. She was going to be a little late to lunch because she desperately needed to relieve herself.

Bristol, Raine, and Idonea were sitting with Kiren on the terrace under a canopy, and all looked up at the approach of Nerthus. Bristol frowned because Nerthus appeared pale, even shaken. Raine, on the other hand, merely sighed while a smile played about Idonea's lips. Nerthus settled into her seat and at first said nothing, not even acknowledging those at the table.

"Is everything all right?" Raine asked.

"The woman, that one in the red armor with the silver hair, she is—? I mean, what is—?" Nerthus stammered, then trailed off. "Who is—?" she began again, once more failing to form a coherent thought.

"Ah," Idonea said, "you met my mother."

If possible, Nerthus grew even paler. "That's your mother?"

"Yes, my mother," Idonea said, then pointed to Raine, "her lover."

Nerthus was still befuddled, knowing there was something important she was missing in that revelation. She struggled, trying to pull the pieces together, and blanched when she did.

"Your mother is a dragon?"

"Yes," Idonea said, "did I fail to mention that? You should feel honored. She rarely has anything to do with mortals."

Nerthus did not feel honored; she felt petrified. That exchange had been more than a warning, it had been a threat. The vial Nerthus wore about her neck held a few drops of Idonea's blood. Mages could be tracked with their own blood and the Empire, at her urging, had been obtaining samples from mages and storing them as a defensive strategy. Despite Nerthus' dislike of magic and mages, that was not why she carried Idonea's blood. Nerthus was so enamored with Idonea she carried the vial so she could find the mage if Idonea ever needed her.

"Well, she didn't eat you, so you must have passed some type of muster," Raine commented.

Kiren giggled. "I like the dragon."

"Talan doesn't like many people, but I think she likes you," Raine said.

Nerthus was finally able to bring her attention back to the matter at hand. The young woman before her appeared happy, healthy, and anything but a prisoner. Although petite, on closer inspection, she was older than Nerthus had first thought. It was the gentleness that permeated her being that gave her such an impression of youth.

"You're the head of the House of Storr?"

That gave Kiren pause. She had always been referred to as the heir to the House of Storr.

"Yes," she said thoughtfully, then more firmly, "yes, I guess I am."

"And you accompany the Alfar Ambassador voluntarily?"

"I do," Kiren said. "I've seen more exciting things since I met her than in all my years before."

"She treats you well?"

A fetching shade of pink crept into Kiren's cheek. "Yes, very well."

Raine hid a smile. Feyden had often expressed disbelief at his sister's constant parade of paramours. He granted she was attractive and powerful, but even that seemed insufficient to explain her ability to juggle so many lovers. Lorifal had pointed out, somewhat indelicately, that she must be really good in bed. Feyden had been horrified and both Raine and Lorifal had burst into laughter. But Raine had to agree with her dwarven friend: from what she had heard, Maeva was very skilled.

"And what are your plans for your land?"

Kiren chewed her lip thoughtfully. "I see no reason to do anything different than my mother. She was very wise. She allowed both the Alfar and Empire access to our holdings. I've leased a parcel in the higher elevations to an Alfar farmer who wants to grow grapes for his winery. And I received a petition from an imperial farmer to graze his sheep in the lowlands, which I'm also inclined to grant. I'll continue to review requests as they come in."

"And you've not received pressure from the Ambassador in these matters?"

"Well it's not her land, now, is it?"

Bristol openly chuckled. There was far more to this little one than met the eye. And he was beginning to think that Maeva had taken on more than she anticipated. He would enjoy telling the Emperor about this conversation. They might have an ally in the enemy's camp.

"When we're finished here," Raine said, "I'll try to convince Maeva to return to the imperial capital to re-open talks. Will you go with her?"

Kiren's eyes glowed at the prospect. "I would like that very much. I've never seen the capital."

"Although the Alfar embassy is very nice, you're welcome to stay at Fireside if you wish."

Kiren had read about the magnificent residence, one that was said to be rivaled only by the imperial palace itself. "That would be wonderful!"

Raine turned to Nerthus. "And there you have it. Kiren's not a prisoner, nor a puppet of the Alfar. She acts of her own free will. Are you satisfied?"

Nerthus had to admit that Raine was right. Although she had come with preconceived notions, this young woman was not the milk-toast she had expected. In fact, there was a steel beneath her gentle demeanor that could prove advantageous to the Empire. Nerthus would watch the girl for a few days, especially around the ambassador, but for now she was satisfied.

"I am."

"Good. Then I suggest you spend the rest of the day partaking of the legendary hospitality of the Ha'kan. Tomorrow there'll be a ceremony and some pageantry, but today is open."

"I have some duties I must attend to this afternoon," Idonea said, "but I'm free this evening if you want a tour. Or something."

Nerthus cleared her throat, coughed, then cleared her throat again. "A tour, or something, would be nice."

Skye walked in on Gimle and Idonea, who were deep in conversation. As much as she was enjoying her lessons with the two mages, today it would be hard to concentrate. There was so much excitement in the capital, and she had passed Dallan and Rika down on the training fields, playfully but fiercely engaged with some imperials and dwarves. It looked like great fun and she walked past wistfully, her only consolation being that Raine was nowhere in sight, which would have been too much to bear.

"Such a look on your face," Idonea said. "And here I thought you were beginning to enjoy your lessons."

"Oh, I am," Skye exclaimed, "it just will be hard to concentrate today."

"The First Scholar and I were discussing some ways we might work around that. But first I want you to practice your invisibility spell. And I want you to sustain it. And I want you to try it on something big."

Skye frowned. She had used the spell only on small objects with very mixed results. Although her endurance had increased, she still struggled.

"Try it on my desk," Gimle suggested, and Skye's frown deepened. The desk of the First Scholar was enormous, carved from a hardwood that was rare and nearly priceless. This made Skye very nervous.

"Go ahead," Idonea encouraged.

Skye calmed herself and focused. She thought of being in the forest, surrounded by trees, a cool breeze flowing over her. She blended into the foliage, and then disappeared.

So did the desk, and Gimle peered over her spectacles. The space flickered as Skye's surprise at her success affected her focus.

"Maintain your concentration," Idonea instructed softly, "and try to relax."

Skye breathed in-and-out mindfully, as her father had instructed her to do when she first learned archery. She could also hear her mother's voice, guiding her to focus. Her bunched shoulders dropped; her features grew peaceful. The spell stabilized and Idonea nodded with approval.

Gimle stopped holding her breath as Skye maintained the spell. Idonea was also maintaining a spell, the cloak that Isleif had taught her. The First Scholar was impressed with both as each was doing something of which she was incapable. In a very Ha'kan way, this did not inspire jealousy or envy, rather only admiration.

A cloud passed over Skye's features, a stray thought or doubt she could not prevent, and the light in the area of the desk shifted, shimmered, then the desk reappeared with a small explosion. It was charred in several places and tendrils of smoke drifted up from the surface.

"What happened?" Skye said, dismayed. She had just destroyed the First Scholar's desk.

"Hmm," Idonea said. "That's interesting."

"Isn't flame a form of Black Magic?" Gimle asked calmly, less concerned about the desk then about the fact that Skye might have just contaminated her skills.

"Yes," Idonea replied, "It usually is. But that wasn't flame, or Black Magic. Light can burn as intensely as fire, and if properly focused, far more so. That was simply a byproduct of the spell." She turned to Skye. "One you're going to have to control if you're going to use this spell on yourself."

"What?" Skye and Gimle said simultaneously.

"I consider that a very successful test," Idonea said. "Well, without the burning part. So, I think it's time you practice this on a live subject."

"Couldn't she use it on a chicken, or something smaller?" Gimle suggested, trying not to sow doubt in Skye's mind. But the doubt was already there, and Skye nodded vigorously.

"Yes, yes, something smaller." She swallowed hard. The thought of burning anything living upset her, let alone herself.

"In practical terms, size matters. But in theoretical terms, it doesn't matter at all," Idonea said off-handedly. "Isleif has proven that after a certain point, magic becomes independent of scale and can replicate without end."

"That doesn't sound logical, or even possible," Gimle said.

"No, it doesn't. But he's quite convinced it's true."

"Has he ever accomplished such a feat?"

"No," Idonea said, "In his calculations, it's only possible with Light Magic. He believes that he and I are powerful enough to push past that tipping point. But he doesn't advise doing so."

"Why is that?"

"It's that last part, 'replicate without end,' that gives him pause. According to his theory, the magic could begin to increase exponentially, setting up a chain reaction that would, well," she said, still discussing the whole matter casually, "just wouldn't stop."

Skye looked at her in horror but Idonea just laughed.

"You're nowhere near the tipping point, little one. We just have to find a way to get you to concentrate."

"You're referring to our earlier conversation," Gimle said.

"Yes, I think that might be the safest way to proceed."

"Very well, come along Skye."

Their conversation was very matter of fact, which is why Skye was more than a little surprised that Gimle was directing her to the adjacent bedroom in that same matter-of-fact manner. She followed obediently out of habit, and Idonea followed her, the slightest trace of a wicked smile on her lips.

Skye was very confused. Gimle turned around and placed her hands on the hem of Skye's shirt.

"Raise your arms," she instructed, and Skye obeyed, still lost. Gimle performed the magic trick of disrobing women that all Ha'kan seemed born with and removed the shirt effortlessly. Skye's cheeks grew very warm.

"What—?"

Idonea settled into the cushioned bench by the doorway and gathered her energy to sustain the cloaking spell. This could take awhile. "Don't mind me."

"Idonea believes that magic and sexual energy are intimately intertwined," Gimle explained, her tone still entirely professional. "Ha'kan research supports this theory. If you wish, I can call a Priestess or one of your cohort in here. I just thought it would be safer if the experiment were conducted with me."

"Safer?" Skye stammered.

The willowy First Scholar gazed down at the beautiful forest sprite of a girl. There was the faintest flicker in her eyes, one that reminded Skye very much of Kara, for it seemed all Ha'kan scholars had the same outward reserve that so artfully concealed the fire within.

"Well," Gimle said, "perhaps that's not my entire motivation."

And then Skye wasn't thinking so much about her studies, or magic, or really anything beyond the slender, lovely woman in front of her. All of the Queen's staff were mesmerizing and had been to Skye from the first day she had met them years before. Gimle had a dreamy, distracted, untouchable air about her that filled Skye with both confusion and longing, a wall of reserve that promised extraordinary things if it were ever breached. Gimle did not move with Senta's strength but acted with just as much confidence and authority. And perhaps even more so, for Gimle's confidence arose from deep knowledge: that very Ha'kan ability to look at a woman and know how inevitable it was that they would wind up in your bed.

"What would you like me to do?" Skye asked softly.

Gimle turned to Idonea. She would not have proposed for Skye to use her abilities this soon, but she trusted Idonea's judgment in all things magical. Idonea would not recommend anything that would hurt Skye or her.

"You've experimented with blindfolds, I assume?" Idonea asked.

That was one of Kara's favorite pastimes, "to limit the visual experience to enhance the other senses," especially touch. She posited that because the blind-folded woman could not see, the anticipation of the touch, and therefore its affect, was magnified. Skye had to agree, at least based on her experience, that Kara was correct.

"Yes," Skye responded.

"Then I want you to pleasure the First Scholar while you're invisible."

Skye swallowed hard and ran her fingers through her hair. She did not see how it was possible that she could sustain the spell and engage in such an overwhelming activity, especially when she had never used the spell solely on herself, doing nothing else at all. Not to mention the fact that she had never had sex with Gimle before, and that was a monumental event.

Gimle could see the doubt in Skye and forcefully suppressed her own. It was all or nothing time.

"Come along, Skye," Gimle said. She moved to the bed, undid the sash at her waist, and dropped the scholar's robe to the floor. And Skye was no longer thinking about magic, for Gimle possessed long limbs and gentle curves, an enticing swell of breasts above sheer undergarments, and soft, pale skin that shimmered in the light. She removed the clasp from her hair and the long, fair strands that were always bound in a braid or pulled back were loosed, the hair surprisingly full given its fineness. And Skye would never look at Gimle the same way, knowing what was concealed beneath her robes.

Idonea herself was distracted, again wondering how her mother or Raine stayed faithful to one another around the Ha'kan. Really, were the circumstances different and the Knight Commander not present, she probably would have begun working her way through the population. She focused.

"Go ahead, Skye," she encouraged.

Skye moved to the bed as Gimle sat on its edge. She so desperately wanted to kiss her and Gimle satisfied that want by pulling her down and kissing her deeply. Skye hungrily returned the kiss, for it was a desire denied for many years, first by her youth, then by her trepidation. And she wanted to kiss all of the skin that had been hidden beneath that robe. Her hand cupped the breasts she had dreamed about while sitting and studying with the First Scholar, and her fingers slipped inside the silk undergarment.

"Wait," Gimle said, exercising all her self-control because she did not want Skye to wait. "You may put your lips there only when I can't see you."

Skye's desire to please the First Scholar was all-consuming, and she barely hesitated before complying. And this time, she did not think of hiding in the forest, or blending in with the foliage, she thought only of how marvelous it would be to have that breast in her mouth and to pleasure Gimle.

And Skye was gone.

Idonea held her breath as she felt the surge of power and sought to balance the cloak against the forces against it. She stabilized the spell and watched the First Scholar closely for signs of success.

Gimle went backward until she was lying in the bed, guided by some unseen force. She had a look of surprise that was transitioning to one of intense pleasure.

"Oh my," she murmured.

And Skye was in heaven. She could do as she wished to the First Scholar and she played and experimented as she never would have in other circumstances. Her lips found every sensitive area, at times leaving a trail so that Gimle could feel her progress, at other times removing her touch so Gimle could not predict where she would go. Skye lightly bit her neck, left a trail of kisses down to one erect nipple, then pulled away for several seconds while Gimle trembled in anticipation. The First Scholar jumped when she felt the light brush of fingertips between her legs and made a soft sound at the sensation. The torturous feathering touch explored each leg, finding the ticklish spot on her hip, and the sensitive spot behind her knee. Skye correctly deduced that Gimle's feet were an erogenous zone for her and gave them extended attention. And then the touch was gone again, for what seemed an eternity as all parts of Gimle twitched with expectation. And it was not the same as being blind-folded, for she could look down at her own body as it was being seduced and see nothing, which was a far more intense experience than being masked.

And then Skye put her mouth between Gimle's legs and the First Scholar gasped, arched, and instantly gave way to the demanding lips and tongue. Although Idonea could not see Skye, it was not difficult to decipher what was occurring. The sexual endurance of the Ha'kan was not exaggerated and Idonea sincerely hoped that Skye would wrap things up because the scene was so arousing, she was struggling to maintain her own spell.

At last the First Scholar came to climax, or perhaps ten or twelve, it was difficult to say, and Skye reappeared as she collapsed on top of her. Idonea was pleased to see that Skye was not on fire or smoking in any manner, at least none that was non-metaphorical. She released her cloaking spell, then released her breath, possibly as spent as the two in the bed.

Gimle stared up at the ceiling while she intertwined her fingers in Skye's hair.

"By the Divine," she murmured, "I would call that a success."

Skye hugged her tightly, barely able to keep her eyes open. She had not felt fatigued at all maintaining the spell and had not really even been thinking about it. But now that it was finished, she was exhausted.

"You'll have to work on her endurance," Idonea said wryly.

Gimle cast the dark-haired mage a glance that was somehow completely professional and utterly erotic at the same time.

"We'll repeat the experiment until the results are perfected."

Idonea entered the guest chambers of the Queen, the one where Raine and Weynild were staying. The two were lying on the couch reading, their limbs intertwined. Even after decades, Idonea was still taken aback at how casually domestic her mother could be around Raine.

Weynild correctly interpreted her daughter's expression. "And so, your experiment was a success?

"To put it mildly," Idonea said. "I got the idea after our conversation about 'magical creatures' and their lack of sexual restraint. Might as well put the flaw to good use. It does seem to be quite the training aid for Skye. Not only was she able to turn herself invisible without mishap, she was able to sustain the spell through the entire escapade. Which was quite lengthy, I might add."

"And did the First Scholar enjoy the lesson?" Raine asked.

"You can't imagine," Idonea said. "I myself am going to have to go find that Knight Commander and release some of my own magical energy."

Weynild returned to her book. "Good idea, my dear. Go fuck your— and our—way into the good graces of the Empire."

Idonea merely laughed and then left to do just that.

"And what do you base these suspicions on?" Maeva asked the Chief of her Security.

"Our envoys have reported the imperials gathering in strategic locations throughout the palace and grounds, talking in low tones and looking about as if surveilling the place."

"Are you sure they're not simply admiring the multitude of beautiful women surrounding them?" Maeva asked, her tone acerbic. "I noticed our own soldiers acting just as 'suspiciously.'"

Faelon retained his composure under the withering assessment. "I have additional reports that the Knight Commander, Nerthus, is acting extremely suspect."

"How so?"

"Despite our efforts to follow her, she's disappeared on several occasions, into areas of the castle we don't have access to, nor does she."

"For example?"

"She was seen in the vicinity of the forum of the Ha'kan princess."

That was unusual, Maeva admitted. She knew how tight security was for the royal family. The Ha'kan were understated about it, but access to the Queen's or Princess's forum was by invitation only. All others were politely but firmly removed by the Royal Guard.

"Anything else?"

"She's been described as flustered, anxious, even unnerved, which is at odds with everything in her dossier."

"Yes, it is," Maeva agreed. Nerthus had been described as cold, inflexible, rigid in temperament, a bitter and outspoken critic of the Alfar. All had been surprised that she had been the one to de-escalate the situation and agree to a meeting in the Ha'kan capital. Such diplomacy was out of character for her, as were her actions now.

"You'll stay on top of this situation," Maeva directed. "Give it your full attention."

Faelon bowed. "Of course, Ambassador. Will you tell anyone else?"

"I'm not sure."

"Are you expecting any more visitors this evening?" Weynild asked.

Raine held her head in her hands, pinched the bridge of her nose, rubbed her eyes, then sat upright.

"I certainly hope not."

Skye had been the first to stop by, hesitantly relaying the rumors she had heard. Raine thanked her for sharing the confidence and told her to stay close on the morrow. Shortly thereafter, Feyden came in and repeated the conversation Lorifal had overheard. They spoke briefly of potential meanings and possible outcomes, and Raine reassured Feyden she would help protect Maeva if needed. Not long after that, Maeva made a surprise appearance herself, related her concerns about the imperials, then left with Raine's assurances that she would act if need be.

"The imperials were already suspicious of the Alfar, and now the Alfar are suspicious of the imperials because the Knight Commander is bed-hopping with my daughter," Weynild said.

"Not really," Raine mused, "from what I can tell they rarely use a bed."

"And suspicions flare between the Ha'kan and Tavinter," Weynild continued, "mild though those suspicions may be."

"Mild, but at an inconvenient time. It's this plot with the Alfar that worries me. It seems the most legitimate concern. Power struggles among the aristocracy are common."

"As are assassinations," Weynild said, "although that's not occurred in decades. And if Maeva is killed during attempts at reconciliation with these other nations, Alfar cooperation will cease to exist."

"And I would say the dwarves have thus far escaped suspicion, but I overheard an imperial say they didn't trust the Dverger because of their close ties to the Alfar."

Weynild leaned down and kissed Raine on the forehead.

"Tomorrow will be an interesting day."

Chapter 9

The training field of the Ha'kan palace was decorated in glorious fashion. Colorful banners bordered the fields and the flags of the Empire, the Alfar, the Dverger, the Tavinter, and the Ha'kan flew on the parapets above. The marble seating area next to the field was packed with spectators, and the grass area below was full of participants. The level between seating areas, the terrace reserved for the Queen and honored guests, was full.

Maeva sat with Kiren, flanked by Edwenil and Faelon. All wore the beautiful garments of the Alfar, Maeva especially splendid in Ambassadorial robes. The Ha'kan dressed according to their castes, the Queen and High Priestess dazzling, the First Scholar a picture of academic grace, the First General magnificent and imposing in full armor. The Dwarves had come in style, all heavily armored in different ceremonial gear, some made of iron, some made of steel, some made of some fascinating amalgams of ore that defied identification. The Tavinter moved about in their polished leather armor, and the imperials had tended to their gear until all gleamed.

Although Skye and Dallan had initially planned to be part of the ceremony, Raine had quietly convinced them to remain in the stands close to the Queen. Although she had not given them a reason, they both complied without question. Rika then bowed out of the exhibition, determined to remain close to her Princess and her friend, and when Senta, who hovered about the Queen, looked on her with approval, she knew she had made a wise decision.

Raine had also quietly asked Lorifal and Feyden to stay close, and alerted Dagna and Elyara that their skills might be needed. Although Raine's manner was utterly calm, all four keyed on Raine's understated warning and took it more seriously for its mildness. They also noted Raine wore her bluish leather armor and had donned a plethora of weapons, including a wicked-looking, folded gadget that attracted a great deal of interest from those who did not know what it was.

Idonea sat near both Knight Commanders, locating herself strategically should either be the intended target. Jorden and Syn sat behind everyone on the terrace and scanned the area with the practiced eyes of master thieves. Raine would glance to them from time-to-time, and Jorden would give a subtle shake of her head, indicating she saw nothing out of the ordinary.

Weynild stood above all, a solitary figure on the upper terrace, scanning the arena with her supernaturally acute vision. She had no indication that today was the day; the assassination could have as easily been attempted in a private chamber in the dark of night. But both she and Raine felt that this was a prime opportunity, that if one of the honored guests could be killed in this very public forum, it would be disastrous.

The exhibition began with great fanfare, and the Ha'kan troops came out in splendid formation, executing intricate battle movements so precise it was a wonder that none of the infantry were trampled by those on horseback. As distracted as Senta was, she still felt pride at the skill of her troops. Bristol was awed by the coordination of the Ha'kan for they moved as a single unit, as communal in battle as they were in all else. He would have to relay this information to the Emperor. Although there had been long-term peace between their nations, it would not hurt to pass on this military intelligence. This emperor had often talked of expanding the Empire. Although the sons and daughters of men outnumbered the Ha'kan almost three to one, it was unlikely they would prevail against such a foe.

Maeva, too, was impressed with the military discipline and coordination of the Ha'kan. It gave her a renewed appreciation of the Tavinter and their young ruler. Although the Alfar possessed military might and numbers equivalent to the Ha'kan, she was not certain the Alfar would have emerged from three years of war with the Ha'kan relatively unscathed, as had the nomadic forest people. Edwenil had little interest in the display as military matters bored her, and therefore she had no grasp of the skill before her. Faelon also tried to act bored, but he understood military tactics and therefore was not successful: the Ha'kan were magnificent. Kiren clapped joyfully at the display, unrestrained in her admiration and Maeva, who would have chastised anyone else, looked upon her fondly.

The Ha'kan exhibition ended to lengthy applause and Senta again felt a surge of pride. Dallan and Rika normally would have led such a series of maneuvers, but their replacements had risen to the task. It was one of the most basic of Ha'kan military philosophies: if a Ha'kan fell in battle, the transition in command was seamless and instantaneous.

It was now the Alfar's turn to impress and they came out on horseback in full pageantry. They wheeled about in splendid fashion while another group scurried about, putting dummies in place for the exercise. The dummies were four deep in a line and "armed" with spears and swords. The Alfar started some distance away, then began charging their mock adversaries at full speed. With a grace and fluidity that seemed impossible, the Alfar drew their bows and, guiding their horses only with their legs, began firing at the dummies as they bore down upon them.

"By the gods," Skye murmured. She knew how difficult it was to fire accurately on horseback and although she thought she could match the feat, she did not know many who could even among the Tavinter. And the Alfar were very accurate, able to draw and fire three times although they were charging full speed and maintaining control of their horses through balance alone. And as they came to the final dummy in the line, it seemed they were too close for a ranged weapon, all flicked the bow around and decapitated the last target with the lower leading edge of the riser.

"That was impressive," Dallan admitted under her breath. The Ha'kan trained with the bow as a melee weapon, but it was an adjunct method at best, a technique of last resort. They emphasized moving to the sword as quickly as possible and therefore trained in that manner. Perhaps they would have to explore this method in greater depth.

Maeva was pleased at the exhibition and leaned over to the Queen. "This is a technique developed by my brother. It's unique in Arianthem."

"It's very impressive," Halla agreed.

"I bet not even that Scinterian could manage that," Faelon said disparagingly, whispering to Edwenil.

Edwenil was still bored. "Probably not. She didn't do a lot on our hunting trip, and she's not doing anything today. I think her skills are overrated."

Raine could hear everything being said about her, but none of these comments mattered. She continued to scan the area, and was filled with a sudden tension. She looked upward to Weynild, who was also scanning the area with renewed intensity. And a jerking movement from Idonea attracted her eye as she, too, sensed something and began to search for it.

Raine did not know why she was moving but her Scinterian instincts took over and she stepped in front of the row of chairs where the Queen and Maeva were seated. In an astonishing move, she pulled the folded object from her belt, violently twisted her wrist, and snapped the bow out to its full length. As she did so, the wickedly sharp leading edge swatted one arrow from the sky as it snapped to the right and another arrow as the second riser snapped to the left. It was a fluid, gorgeous, deadly maneuver that saved the lives of those behind her.

The terrace exploded into pandemonium as Senta and the Royal Guard surrounded the Queen, High Priestess, and First Scholar. Skye drew her bow and Dallan her sword while Rika moved in front of both of them. Faelon sought to move closer to Maeva but he was blocked by Feyden who had drawn his sword and pointed it at Faelon's throat. Maeva clutched Kiren to her while drawing a dagger, uncertain who to point it at. It briefly hovered in Lorifal's direction, but he had his back to her and seemed to have inserted himself in some protective manner between her and Edwenil.

Idonea had leaped to her feet when the arrows flitted in and Nerthus, although completely confused, moved to protect her. Idonea needed no protection, but welcomed the proximity because now the Knight Commander was close enough for Idonea to protect both her and Bristol. Both imperials had drawn their greatswords, which now hovered uncertainly in every direction at the unseen threat.

But it was not unseen to Raine, who had unerringly tracked the source of the arrows. Idonea yelled to Raine to warn her of the presence of at least two more assassins, but the warning was not needed. The wrist twisted, the bow twirled with a violent snap and two more arrows were swatted from the sky with deadly precision. And then the bow came upward, an arrow was notched with supernatural speed, and the projectile was loosed with such force and accuracy that it disappeared from the Scinterian weapon and appeared far off in the distance as a tiny dark figure on the upper, outer wall stiffened, then toppled from the parapet, falling to the ground several stories below.

Raine was already loosing another arrow in a completely different direction, seemingly without effort and without taking aim. Again, the arrow flew with supernatural accuracy and plucked a figure from a spot on the upper wall. It toppled to the ground. The wrist twisted, the bow snapped, and two more arrows were swatted from the ground as the remaining assassins turned their attention to the creature who was impossibly taking them down. Although they had fired an equal distance, they were using crossbows, a weapon producing greater force and accuracy over long distances. They also had fired from concealment, remaining perfectly still, taking ample time to aim. The Scinterian, on the other hand, was using a standard bow, if the ancient weapon could be called that, was under fire, and had not stopped moving. And she was destroying them.

Raine sprinted to the edge of the terrace and launched herself from the platform with an incredible leap. It appeared she was jumping into thin air and would suffer a terrible fall, but then a colossal hot wind swept through the crowd and an enormous shadow fell over all as a fiery red dragon swooped down. Raine landed crouched on the dragon's back as it glided low and scrambled toward the neck as a thrust of the wings sent them skyward. She positioned herself between two bony plates and raised her bow once more. She could see a figure garbed in black racing along the parapet. If her suspicious were correct, they had only seconds before the assassins escaped. She steadied herself by flexing the strong muscles in her legs, leaned sideways, and fired from a ridiculously awkward position. And the black figure staggered, stumbled, slowed, then crumpled to the ground.

And the dragon wheeled about in a tight, descending spiral, the massive jaws plucking the last figure from the wall and clamping down. The figure screamed and it was difficult to tell if it was male or female. Raine was close enough to see the strange black garb that clothed the figure from head-to-toe. Then black smoke began to pour from the body, and it dissolved into embers and ash that flowed back upon Raine.

The dragon wheeled about once more, scanning the area, then swooped down to briefly hover over the field while Raine alighted. The ground shook as the dragon landed, then the massive creature disappeared into a brilliant flash of yellow light. Weynild stood in her human form, a look of distaste on her features as Raine approached.

"I'll not get that foulness from my mouth any time soon," she said.

"So that was what I thought it was?" Raine asked.

"Yes," Weynild said, then discreetly spit to the side. "Unfortunately." She looked toward the crowd standing on the terrace above. "I'm going to fly around the capital to ensure there are no more. I'll return shortly."

"I'll try and get this chaos settled down."

Weynild transformed and leapt skyward. Raine walked across the field with a growing accompaniment of Ha'kan and Alfar. One of the Ha'kan Royal Guard fell into step beside Raine.

"We went to retrieve the bodies where they fell from the wall, but there was nothing but a pile of scorched earth and ash in an outline."

"That doesn't surprise me," Raine said without explanation. She started up the stairs to the terrace. Everyone was still in full alert and there were many weapons hovering in dangerous positions. Accusations were flying, doing as much damage as the potential of the poised weapons.

"What's the meaning of this?" Maeva demanded, uncertain who to ask, so turning to her brother.

"These two," Feyden said scathingly, pointing his sword at Edwenil and Faelon, "are plotting against you."

"What?" Faelon demanded, his voice almost shrill. "This is the imperials' doings. That Knight Commander plotted the whole thing!"

Nerthus stepped forward, her greatsword thrusting toward the elven security guard. "You hold your tongue, you pointy-eared bastard!"

Fortunately, Idonea was in position to grasp the blade of the sword, an act that would have sliced any normal creature's hand in two. But Idonea's motion was not physical but magical and she held the massive blade in check, secure between her finger and thumb.

"You will calm yourself," she murmured to Nerthus, and against her will, Nerthus complied.

"I can't believe any amongst my people would do this," Skye said, distraught.

"There's no evidence this was your people," the Queen began, but Senta interrupted.

"If it was your people," she said, "we know it wasn't you."

This did not soothe Skye in any way and surprised the Queen. She had been aware of Senta's heightened vigilance, but apparently things were worse than she thought. Now she wondered what Senta knew.

"I tell you it's the imperials," Faelon insisted, pointing at Nerthus, "That one has been sneaking around since she got here!"

"Enough!"

Raine's tone of voice was commanding and all fell silent. "You will sheath your weapons now," she said, her tone quietly seething, "and I will kill the first who draws again."

Slowly, all put their weapons away.

"We'll gather in the Ha'kan Council Room."

It was a somber and angry group that made its way to the amphitheater where the Ha'kan discussed important affairs. The marble seats were crowded with Ha'kan and Alfar troops who sought to be close to their lieges. The Dverger and imperials were far fewer in number, but they, too, found space where they huddled with their own. Others stood on the upper platform, between the stone-carved columns.

At the council table, Senta hovered behind the Queen who took her place at the head. Gimle and Astrid sat on each side while Dallan, Skye, and Rika sat in the first row nearby. Lorifal and Feyden flanked Maeva, who kept Kiren close by her side. Edwenil and Faelon were a short distance away, and Idonea sat between them and the very surly imperials. Jorden and Syn sat next to Skye in the front row. Raine sat in the middle of the table, brooding and lost in thought while the quiet discussion and bickering continued.

"I can't believe any of my people would do this," Skye mumbled.

Rika put her arm around her shoulders. "It's too soon to place blame. Give Raine a chance to sort this out."

Jorden agreed. "This doesn't bear the mark of the Tavinter."

Feyden leaped to his feet and pointed his finger angrily at Edwenil and Faelon. "You two are responsible for this! Lorifal heard you plotting in the hallway, discussing plans to overthrow my sister. 'I flirt with her brother to allay suspicion.' You two are traitors!"

"What?" Edwenil said, shocked to hear her words thrown back at her. "No, you don't understand!"

Feyden would have drawn his sword again had it not been for Raine's vehement warning. "What is there to understand? You wanted to be Directorate but Maeva would have easily defeated you. What better way to assume the position than have her assassinated?"

"That's not true! You don't understand!" Edwenil repeated frantically, unable to explain herself other than by repeating this same phrase.

Faelon, although lesser rank than Edwenil, could stand no more. He jumped to his feet. "She was flirting with you to hide her love for me!"

Maeva sighed with disgust and pinched the bridge of her nose with her fingertips. This was all very sordid and melodramatic, unworthy of the Alfar. She would have preferred an assassination attempt; it would have been more dignified.

"What?" Feyden asked, confused. "What are you talking about?"

"We wish to marry," Faelon said defiantly, "we were going to elope."

Comprehension was slow to dawn, but it did at last. Feyden sat back down, his anger and distrust dissolving into mere disbelief. It seemed Raine also understood the oblique explanation and turned to the Ha'kan and the imperials.

"By Alfar tradition, all marriages between the nobility must be approved by the Directorate."

Maeva's tone was scathing as she addressed Edwenil and Faelon. "Did you think I was unaware of your indiscretions? Did you even think to ask before you engaged in this subversion? Granted it's not a favorable match for your House," she said, speaking to Edwenil, "as Faelon is of low rank. But you overestimate my interest in your affairs if you think I would deny you."

She turned away from both of them. "We'll speak no more of this tawdry matter in public. Both of you will be punished for this humiliation."

Raine returned to her brooding. Her thoughts were tangled and unclear, unfocused. The white dragon's words swirled through her head and some epiphany was close to surfacing when Edwenil shrilly interrupted, seeking to deflect attention from herself.

"Well what about the Imperial?" she demanded, pointing at Nerthus. "She's been sneaking about, acting suspicious. What of her?"

Nerthus turned bright red, part from anger, part from the knowledge of what she had actually been doing. Idonea grasped her arm, calming her.

"Oh, that," Idonea said, "we were fucking."

The startling comment elicited a wide range of responses. A gasp from Bristol, a snort of laughter from Lorifal, a delicate clearing of the throat from Queen Halla, a sardonic look from Raine, and a short "hmm," from

Maeva that communicated mild disbelief coupled with a slight uplifting of her opinion of the Knight Commander. That did explain a lot.

The humorous, inappropriate admission served its intended purpose, however, and de-escalated the situation. The mood in the room went from volatile anger back to somber, quiet confusion.

Raine returned to the jumble of thoughts in her head. Again, the white dragon's words began to tumble about as some thought or idea desperately tried to surface in the mental maelstrom.

"Those were no ordinary killers," Raine murmured.

"They weren't even ordinary assassins."

The commanding voice came from the entrance and all of the Ha'kan stood as an elegant silver-haired woman strode into the hall. All others followed suit. Although the dragon had been present in the capital, most had not met her. Those that had met Talan'alaith'illaria were thrilled by her presence, those that had not were stunned into fearful awe. Her fiery armor shimmered in the light, dreadful and beautiful all at the same time. She was imposing under normal circumstances; in a formal setting, she was majestic. Few mortals were blessed with the company of one of the twelve Ancients, and this was the greatest of the twelve. Queen Halla rendered a deep curtsy, Maeva bowed low in the most reverent gesture of the Alfar, and all others went to a knee, even Idonea, who would give her mother the respect due on formal occasion. The only one who remained standing was Raine, who waited for her lover to approach, took her hand, and kissed it in a gesture more worshipful than all others combined. The dragon's gold eyes drifted over the assembly as they rose and retook their seats, then returned to Raine.

"Were they what I think they were?" Raine asked.

"Yes," Weynild replied with distaste, "vampyre."

"That's not good," Jorden muttered, probably the only other person present who understood the significance. A quick glance from Raine told her they would speak of this later.

"If they're professional assassins," Senta asked, "then how are we to know who hired them? It could have been anyone here."

A general rumble of protest and accusation began to rise from the crowd, one immediately silenced by a mere glance from a pair of glowing, amber eyes. Weynild turned again to Raine.

"Tell me what you're thinking."

The wise presence of her lover helped Raine focus. "The white dragon said 'that which seems to matter doesn't at all,'" she said slowly as the epiphany struggled to surface once more.

"And what mattered most to you?" Weynild prompted.

"The target," Raine said, thinking aloud, her certainty growing, "knowing the target was most important, even more important than knowing the aggressor. Only by knowing the target could I prevent the assassination."

"And why doesn't that matter now?" Weynild again prompted.

It finally came together.

"There was no single target."

Raine pointed to Maeva. "The first arrow was fired at you," she said, recreating the events in her mind, "but the second arrow was for you," she said, pointing at Queen Halla. "The third and fourth arrows could have been for either of you," she said, pointing at Skye and Dallan, "and the fourth and fifth was for one, or both, of you," she said, gesturing to Bristol and Nerthus. "You were likely targets of last choice because of your heavy armor."

"Why target all of us?" Queen Halla asked.

"Because the goal wasn't to kill any one of you," Raine said, "that was simply means to an end."

"So, what was the goal?" Maeva asked.

"To sow the seeds of distrust," Weynild said, "to destroy this alliance before it was born."

Silence settled on the assembly at the portent of these words.

"So," Maeva said slowly, "although we all had a motive, it wasn't any of us?"

Raine looked around, assessing the cast of characters one-by-one, weighing each. "No," she said at last, satisfied and relieved, "it wasn't any of you."

"It was someone who wants this alliance to fail," Weynild said. "Someone who'll benefit from the return of the Hyr'rok'kin."

"Is it Hel?" Idonea asked, eliciting several gasps from the crowd.

"No, I don't think so." Raine looked to Weynild for confirmation. "It's not her style. She'd rather destroy the lot of us all at once."

"Well, she doesn't really want to 'destroy' you," Idonea pointed out.

Raine cast her a dark look. "My fate will be worse than death." She returned to her earlier musings. "The white dragon said, 'who else has the most to gain?' I thought her phrasing strange, but she meant who else other than Hel, would have the most to gain."

"Who had the most to gain during the Great War?"

The voice was soft in the cavernous hall, but it did not waver. And it was addressed to the only occupant of the room that had actually fought in the Great War. All eyes turned toward Kiren.

"You're very wise, little one," Weynild said, answering the question directed at her. "That occurred to me. And you may be right." She addressed Raine. "I'll return shortly."

The assembly rose as one at the dragon's departure, then resettled, unwilling to adjourn just yet. Raine sat down heavily, drained.

"I would like to thank you," Queen Halla, "you saved my life and prevented disaster. Again."

"You're most welcome, my Queen," Raine said.

"And I owe you my thanks as well," Maeva added, "you also saved me. I admit I've never seen anything like that bow, or the way you use it."

"Where do you think I learned it from?" Feyden murmured.

Raine gave Feyden a tired smile as she responded to Maeva. "The weapon was my father's. Very ancient. And Feyden never would have forgiven me if I let something happen to you."

"Raine," Queen Halla asked, "can you explain the reference to the Great War? There are many myths and legends of what happened, but also many conflicting accounts."

"Kiren?" Raine prompted. "You're the one who made the connection. Would you like to share your thoughts?"

Kiren blushed, pleased at the recognition. "I loved tales of the Great War, so I studied and cross-referenced as many sources as I could find. Those written in Ancient Elvish, although brief, were the most detailed."

"The cause of the War was never fully understood. Many speculated it was a battle between the gods themselves, a conflict over the boundaries of the different realms. Hyr'rok'kin began spewing from the earth by the tens of thousands, then hundreds of thousands."

Many in the room blanched at the thought of hundreds of thousands of Hyr'rok'kin. Even a handful could be devastating. An army of that size would be unstoppable.

"How could the people of that time stand against so many of those monsters?" Senta asked.

"They couldn't," Kiren said simply. "They were facing annihilation. The only race able to fight with any success were the Scinterians, and even their losses were horrific."

"But I bet they enjoyed it," Raine murmured, a fierce, far-off look in her eye. Several pairs of eyes slid uneasily in her direction, and Maeva gained new insight into the lethality of the creature next to her. As impressive as

Raine's feats had been that day, Maeva had the suspicion they might have been effortless for the warrior.

Kiren smiled. "Yes, by all accounts, the Scinterians loved battle. They did what they could for the other races, and all banded together as one. Several races disappeared in that era, and a few others were born from these bonds. Light and Dark Magic was very strong, and mystical creatures of both roamed Arianthem: demi-gods, sprites, nymphs, witches, all were numerous."

"They grow in numbers now," Idonea said, "just like then."

"So, what happened?" Queen Halla asked. "What was the deciding factor that turned the tide?"

Kiren looked to Raine, and Raine spoke the answer.

"The dragons."

Kiren was sad and thoughtful. "I believe that's why there are so few of them left. The twelve Ancients were fragmented in opinion. Some wished to stay out of the conflict, and some wished to join the forces of darkness. Some wished to merely benefit from the chaos and destruction. But one dragon's voice rose above all others, one who sought to fight the black forces and come to the aid of Arianthem. Many of the council sided with her, and many of the lesser dragons followed her as well. But still it was not enough as the remaining dragons sided with the Hyr'rok'kin."

Kiren was silent for a moment, and Lorifal could barely contain himself. "What happened next, lass?"

"The dragon, the one that opposed the Hyr'rok'kin, had a most brilliant and unorthodox plan. She approached the Scinterians, the ultimate dragon slayers, her most bitter and ferocious foe, and she proposed an alliance."

A smile played about Raine's lips. "And the Scinterians accepted," she said, taking up the thread of the story, "leading to the greatest union of all time."

"That union," Kiren continued, "between the Scinterians and the dragons, determined the outcome of the Great War. And the link between the two was unbreakable, some Scinterians going so far as to undergo the ceremony of binding, something that had only been accomplished between dragonkind."

"The ceremony of binding?" Gimle asked. "I've read of this. Isn't that the interlocking of souls?"

"Yes," Kiren said, "The life-force of one will not leave without the other."

Raine felt the weight of Idonea's gaze upon her. The thoughtful speculation on her face told Raine this was a conversation they would be having later.

"And so, the dragons and the Scinterians drove the Hyr'rok'kin back into the Underworld, but both suffered terrible losses. The Scinterians were so few in number they ceased to exist within a few generations, and the dragons almost disappeared. The people of Arianthem, however, recovered and then thrived."

Complete silence settled on the assembly as they contemplated this somber tale and the sacrifices that had been made. They looked with different eyes upon the Scinterian in their midst, the only survivor of the mythic race that had been a large part of their salvation.

"So," Gimle said, returning to the original question, "you believe it's the dragons who wish the return of the Hyr'rok'kin?"

"It's possible," Raine said, "there are more of them left than you would think, especially the lesser. And they're the only ones who'll benefit from such an onslaught."

"Raine," Queen Halla asked quietly, "what was the name of the dragon who spoke up, the one who opposed the Hyr'rok'kin and created the alliance with the Scinterians?"

"Her name," Raine said, her eyes burning with intensity, "was Talan'alaith'illaria." The words, although quietly spoken, rang out in the immense hall. "Although you have all forgotten, there's a reason why you revere the Queen of Dragons above all others."

Again, the great hall settled into silence, but this time it was filled with electricity and did not last long. Queen Halla rose gracefully from her seat.

"Raine, although, the Ha'kan and Tavinter are already sworn to the service of Talan, I renew this vow. We'll also come to the aid of all who serve her."

Maeva also stood. "The Alfar will match this vow. We'll provide whatever forces you require, and if called to aid, we'll fight anywhere." Her eyes flicked to the imperials, and Bristol took his cue.

"Raine," Bristol said, "Dagna and I've already followed you to the Gates of the Underworld and will do so again. The Emperor gave us," he nodded to Nerthus, "the task of ensuring the safety of the heir to the House of Storr. But we were given a secondary, secret charge on this mission, that if circumstances were favorable, we could verbally enter into treaty, which he would ratify in writing upon our return. We do so now, vowing the service of the Empire to you and Talan, and providing aid to all who serve you."

"And the Emperor will listen to you?" Maeva asked.

"He will listen to her," Bristol said, again nodding to Nerthus. "She's his right hand."

"Really?" Maeva said, revising her opinion of the Knight Commander once more.

"He'll sign the treaty," Nerthus said with confidence.

Lorifal took this opportunity to interject, speaking to Raine. "And if you do go back to the Gates of the Underworld," he said, patting Feyden on the back, "you're not going without us."

"I thank you all," Raine said, "and I ask that whatever differences remain among you, you settle quickly, knowing that they're so very small compared to what we face. And although this has been a long, strange day, our enemies have failed, because where they sought to sow discord, they've created only unity."

A great cheer went up in the hall, and the celebration in the Ha'kan palace would spill out into the streets of the capital and carry on long into the night.

Raine briefly joined the festivities, then retired to her chambers. As she had anticipated, soon there was a knock on her door.

"Come."

Idonea entered, her silken robes flowing behind her, gently swirling as if a physical manifestation of the magic that swirled about her.

"The answer is yes," Raine said without prompting.

Idonea paused, digesting the blunt admission.

"So, you're bound to my mother."

"Yes," Raine said, straightening a coverlet. "She insisted prior to our quest twenty years ago. I didn't wish it for obvious reasons. Your mother, barring violent death, is immortal and although I'll likely live a very long time, I will eventually die."

"And then she'll die."

"I imagine so," Raine said, "my soul can't leave this realm without hers. So, I protested. But she asked me if I wished to live without her, which of course I denied, and then she asked how could I expect different of her?"

Idonea sat down on the couch and Raine settled across from her.

"So how exactly does this work, this interlocking of souls?"

"I'm not entirely sure," Raine said. "But neither life force will leave until the power of the other is exhausted. Although it's more likely this will aid me, there were times in the Great War where Scinterians were able to save their dragon brethren."

"If you had told me this twenty years ago, I would have thought my mother a fool. But now that I know you, I don't think this is as one-sided a bargain as you believe."

"Thank you," Raine said, a slight smile on her lips. "I pray that I'm strong enough to save her should the time come."

Idonea pondered this revelation. Her mother always acted with a myriad of motives. Although she knew her love for Raine was sufficient to engage in such an act, she also knew her mother saw far into the future. She wondered how much that discernment had played into this decision.

The sound of leathery wings intruded upon her thoughts, then the slight shake of the rock solid terrace told her that her mother had arrived. Weynild pushed through the stained-glass doors. She came up behind Raine, ran her long fingers through her hair, then bent down to kiss the lips her young love proffered.

"And were you able to settle everyone down?"

"Better than that," Raine answered, "Kiren told so lyric a story of the Great War, they've all sworn their undying loyalty to you."

"Hmmph. I spent centuries hoping they would forget me, now it'll all be stirred up again."

"It's all for a purpose, my love. I think they'll settle their differences now. Even the Alfar and imperials have proposed a tentative pact."

Another knock on the door interrupted their conversation.

"Come," Raine said.

The Lady Jorden flowed into the room. Jorden looked completely different depending on whether she was in the role or an imperial noblewoman or "Lagmann," the head of the Guild of Thieves. Now she looked wholly the noblewoman, in a beautiful green gown that highlighted the startling blue-green eyes that gazed appreciatively on both Raine and Weynild, then lingered on Idonea. Idonea took note of the gaze, thinking she might accept that implied invitation sometime in the future. Although Jorden and Syn were a couple, it was evident they welcomed others to their shared bed.

Weynild gave her daughter a long look as Jorden sat down on the couch next to her, but Idonea remained impenitent, mirth in her dark eyes. Raine did not waste time with trivialities.

"I imagine you have contacts in the Assassins Guild?"

"Of course," Jorden said, "we collaborate at times. They may have need of a simple theft, no death involved, and we occasionally need to 'send a message.' I prefer my people specialize in thievery, so it's a simple matter to exchange favors among guilds."

Jorden's tone grew serious. "But these are not normal guild assassins."

"No," Raine said, "they were vampyre."

Raine waited to see if Jorden truly understood the significance of the identification.

"Then they're from the Shadow Guild."

She understood. The Shadow Guild was a guild-within-a-guild, the very upper elite of the Guild of Assassins. All were required to become vampyre. Their existence was a jealously guarded secret, and those who knew of them did not speak of them because they were likely to disappear shortly after the conversation.

"I hate vampyre," Idonea muttered.

"Have you ever dealt with the Shadow Guild?" Raine asked.

"No, I've never had that high profile a target. And I'm not sure they would respond even to my request. From what I've heard, their clientele is very limited and very exclusive. And they scorn money, so the payment must be something they want."

"And what is it they want?" Weynild asked, speaking for the first time.

"Again, I repeat only rumors. But sometimes a rare artifact, a priceless scroll, always something to do with power."

"And who would be able to hire the Shadow Guild?"

Jorden shook her head. "Very few. I'm not sure they would respond to a request from the Emperor himself, and they might kill him for daring to ask. For daring to acknowledge their existence. Even with the dignitaries here, I'm not certain anyone has that kind of pull, with the possible exception of the people in this room."

"So, the client has to be enormously powerful and possess something the Guild wants," Raine mused, "so once again, the dragons are a prime suspect. Thank you, Jorden, you've confirmed my suspicions."

Jorden let herself out, and Idonea rose to follow her.

"Idonea," Weynild said, a note of warning in her voice, "don't break the Knight Commander's heart before the treaty is signed."

"Oh mother," Idonea said over her departing shoulder.

When the door closed, Raine stood and went to the bedroom. She disrobed under Weynild's admiring gaze and climbed into bed. Weynild blew a breath into the fireplace, retracted her armor and joined her. The two were intertwined, content for the moment just to lie warm in the soft bed.

"You were splendid today," Weynild said, "perfection."

"Ah yes, one more reason why we're a matched pair." Raine said. "Death and destruction always arouse you."

"And you're so very skilled in bringing about both," Weynild said, kissing her deeply. She felt the body come to life beneath her fingertips and knew they would not be talking long.

"Of course, now the Shadow Guild will be coming for you," Weynild continued, kissing her neck, "they're few in number and you killed four of them today."

"Let them come," Raine murmured, her own hands and lips beginning to explore. "I'll kill them all. How arousing would that be?"

Weynild rolled her onto her back, pressing her long frame to her, breasts tantalizingly close to her lips and hips firmly between her legs.

"Let me show you."

Chapter 10

The sun rose in a pastel pink sky streaked with yellow ribbons. Queen Halla had arisen early and was joined by her staff for a light breakfast on the terrace. The air was chilled, and all but Senta sat with warm blankets on their legs. Halla could see across the bridge to where Dallan and her staff were also gathering for an early meal. Dallan strode over to greet her mother with a light kiss, then returned to Rika, Lifa, Kara, and Skye.

Senta took a sip of strong, black tea. Her attention was drawn to the sentries on the distant castle gate. She was too far away to hear what they were saying, but there was some kind of commotion with a great deal of gesticulation and excitement. The excitement appeared to increase, and word was being passed from person-to-person as guards ran from the gates to sound the alarm. Senta stood, concerned. They had numerous sentries patrolling the outer reaches and the Tavinter were unparalleled in their ability to detect a threat. But something seemed to have penetrated that net of safety.

The tumult below grew as did Senta's concern. Something was coming, and it was coming fast. Finally, a guard was close enough that Senta was able to make out her words.

"A dragon is coming! A black dragon is coming!"

Senta turned to seek out Raine, but Raine was already there with Talan at her side. Both were dressed in full armor, but neither was perturbed. Talan's amber eyes swept the horizon.

"A black dragon is coming," Senta said, addressing them both.

"I know," Talan said, "I summoned him."

This revelation calmed the anxiety of the royal staff but heightened the excited tension in the air. The younger Ha'kan and Skye joined them from the adjacent terrace.

"Did I hear that a dragon is approaching?" Dallan asked.

"Yes," Senta replied, "but Talan has summoned him."

Raine and Talan moved to the stone railing and stood side-by-side, waiting. Idonea joined them while the Ha'kan stood back respectfully. A large cohort of elves had also spilled from Maeva's wing, and the Royal Guard allowed Maeva to pass onto the Queen's terrace where she joined Halla.

"I heard yelling," Maeva said.

"Look, there," Gimle pointed, "in the clouds."

At first it was just a black form, one that could be mistaken for a large bird at an illusory close range. But as it continued to grow, the unique shape and movement of the leathery wings became distinct, the size became evident, and the identification unmistakable: it was an enormous dragon, almost as large as Talan herself. The ebony scales came into sharp relief, the spikes and talons were visible in full detail, and the creature wheeled about the Ha'kan capital, letting loose an earth-shattering roar that terrified all below.

Except Idonea, who muttered under her breath. "He's such a show-off."

It did not affect Raine, either, who crossed her arms over her chest in silent agreement. Weynild simply watched impassively as the drake wheeled about in a tight turn, pulled up with a great thrust of wings, then alighted gracefully on the terrace before her, causing only a slight shake of the palace.

A brilliant flash of red light encompassed the dragon as it transformed, shrinking down into human form.

Raine sighed aloud.

The man before them was gorgeous, raven-black hair, black eyes, a sensual mouth that curved into a wicked grin. He was dressed in an elegant black ensemble, fine black boots, a silken black shirt, exquisitely woven black breeches, and a flowing black cape that fluttered in the slight wind as he approached Talan. He stopped before her and gave an elaborate bow, the gesture so effusive it was dangerously close to mockery. The mischief in his eyes, however, belied any disrespect, and truly, this was exactly what Talan expected of him.

"You called?"

"Yes," Talan said drily, "I did." She held out her hand, giving tacit permission for a more informal greeting, and he immediately complied, putting his hands about her waist, pressing himself to her and kissing her cheek, purposely just catching the corner of her mouth. It was a very sensual greeting, but everything the man did was charged with sexual energy. His gaze, his movement, his voice, everything about him gave the impression of a creature intent on satisfying his own carnal desires. And there was an arrogant certainty of skill that implied the needs of others would probably, if incidentally, be satisfied as well.

The man stepped back as Talan seemed unmoved, even amused by the inappropriate greeting. Raine merely sighed, which brought those glowing black eyes around to her.

"Raine," he breathed out, the warm air filled with his lust and longing. He assessed the full length of her body, starting at the fair hair and traveling slowly all the way down, then making a languorous return trip that settled on her lips. He embraced her, not so bold as to kiss those lips lest she remind him that Scinterians were once dragon slayers, but bold enough to press himself against her for quite some time. Surprisingly, Talan did not respond other than to roll her eyes.

Queen Halla approached uncertainly, trailed by her staff. The man released Raine as Talan spoke.

"Your majesty, this is Drakar'athal'illaria."

"My son."

This elicited several gasps of surprise for a multitude of reasons, not least among them his scandalous behavior. He bowed in a chivalrous manner, his appreciation for the bevy of beauties before him pronounced. One in particular caught his eye and he moved to her in delight.

"Idonea," he exclaimed, then took her in his arms and delivered a passionate, lingering, romantic kiss that caused much consternation in the onlookers. Idonea did not struggle, and even seemed to return the kiss.

"They are siblings, are they not?" the Queen murmured.

"Yes," Talan said, even drier than before, "half, to be precise. There's a reason I've kept them apart their whole lives."

A mere clearing of Talan's throat was enough to separate the two, although Drakar's reluctance was evident.

"Drakar, behave yourself. You're scandalizing even the very tolerant Ha'kan."

"Apologies, mother," he gave Idonea another searing glance. "You know how much I adore my little sister."

"And my apologies," Talan said, addressing the Queen, "I should have warned you. But Drakar was surprisingly responsive this time. Between paramours?" she asked him.

"I always respond to your summons," Drakar insisted. "But yes, my schedule is a little open at the moment."

"Your Majesty," Talan said, "I would speak with my son alone, if you don't mind. And I'll send word later."

"Of course," Halla said, "we await your direction."

Talan and Raine started for the stained-glass door that led to their chambers, no question that "alone" included Raine.

"Idonea?" Talan said over her shoulder. "Why don't you come, too? That is, if Drakar can keep his hands off you long enough to have a conversation."

"No promises," Drakar muttered, "I am my mother's son."

Drakar examined the Ha'kan décor with approval, especially the enormous bed.

"The Ha'kan certainly have their priorities straight. Alas, in all my years, I've only been successful on a handful of occasions in seducing them, and I had to shape-shift into a woman to do so."

Idonea patted his cheek as she walked by. "I'm sure you made a very pretty woman."

"I was gorgeous if you must know. I had breasts the size of watermelons."

Drakar sprawled onto the couch and Raine sat across from him where she was joined by Idonea. Weynild preferred to stand.

"Drakar, how many of the twelve Ancients remain?"

Drakar felt this was a test of sorts as he had no doubt his mother knew the answer to the question she posed.

"Well, let's see. Six were killed during the Great War. This one over here," he said, nodding at Raine, "knocked off poor Ragnar twenty years ago. And you did kill dear old Dad right after the war, shortly after my birth," Drakar said breezily.

"So, three."

"Yes. And yourself for a total of four."

"Hmm," Weynild, "have you seen any of the others?"

"By the gods, no," Drakar said, "the Ancients are a crotchety lot, grumpy, ill-tempered, arrogant...," he paused sheepishly, "present company excepted, of course."

"Of course," Weynild said, falling into silence.

"How many of those that remain sided with you in the Great War?" Raine asked.

"One," Weynild replied, confirming Drakar's hunch that she already knew the answer to the question she asked. "And two who sided with darkness. I wouldn't be surprised if one or both are behind the assassination attempt. It's much like them to skulk about in the shadows and hire others, to disrupt rather than confront."

"What do you think they have that the Shadow Guild wants?" Raine mused.

"I can't imagine," Weynild said in a tone that caught Raine's attention. Somehow, she thought her love might have a pretty good idea what the Shadow Guild wanted.

"Drakar," Weynild continued, "you still move amongst dragonkind. Have you heard anything?"

"Well...."

"This should be good," Idonea said.

"Not too long ago I spent some time with a pretty little thing, a lesser dragon who hadn't the slightest idea who I was. After repeatedly engaging in 'relations,' to my dismay, she was talkative. I nearly dumped her on the spot, but she began speaking in an irritating, conspiratorial manner, trying to regain my attention. I thought at first she was just being melodramatic, but her degree of detail made me think twice."

"And what did she say?"

"She began talking about how the dragons would once again rule the mortal realm when the Hyr'rok'kin invasion began."

"I see," Weynild said, again falling into silence.

"How did your little fling end?" Raine prompted.

"My first impulse was to kill her, of course," Drakar said with a nonchalance reminiscent of his mother, "but then I thought she might be useful sometime in the future. So, I gave her a night to remember, then sent her on her way."

"Good boy," Weynild murmured.

"Well, this complicates things," Idonea said.

"It does indeed," Weynild commented, "Hel will be almost impossible to battle. The dragons will make it worse. They're devious and will do all they can to disrupt this newfound unity. If they involve themselves directly, especially the elders and the Ancients, there are few that can stand against them."

"Other dragons can," Raine said, "just like in the Great War." She did not like where this was going. "Which means you and I are going to be separated again, very soon."

"Yes," Weynild said, "I'll have to go to rally my kind. You need to track down the head of the Shadow Guild and convince her to cease her meddling."

"Her?"

The word hung in the air, the implication obvious. Once again, Weynild knew more than she was revealing, including the identity of the head of the Shadow Guild. But the dragon's ambiguity was never due to a lack of trust, always due to a greater purpose. Raine knew this.

"Yes, 'her.' And you'll have greater success than I."

"If you didn't love me so, I'd think you toy with me, sending me out on these quests, always in the dark."

"Perhaps I just like to set you loose and watch you kill things," Weynild said, bending down to kiss Raine's hair. Raine clasped the hand on her shoulder.

"Well, I enjoy that, too."

"They really are a perfect match," Drakar said to Idonea, shaking his head. "Aren't they?"

"Disgustingly so," Idonea agreed.

Weynild resumed her role as sentry on the parapets of the Ha'kan palace, returning to her solitude. Her children stood a terrace away, standing entirely too close to one another, engaged in animated, playful conversation. Weynild's amber gaze would at times slide in that direction, and Drakar would shift to a more appropriate spacing. This would last only a short time until Weynild looked away and then the two were on top of one another again. Weynild sighed, relieved that the Knight Commander was currently occupied.

Raine went to the conference room and briefed a small group consisting of the Queen and her staff, Maeva and hers, Feyden, Lorifal, Bristol, Dagna, Elyara, and the fortuitously occupied Nerthus. She was vague on the Shadow Guild as those who spoke of such things placed themselves in danger. She had no concerns for herself; she just did not want to burden anyone else. She simply explained that Talan would be setting out for the mountains to seek her kind, and she herself would be seeking out the assassins.

"You're not going without us," Lorifal said, smacking Feyden on the back.

Feyden grunted at the impact. "The dwarf is right. We're going."

"I welcome your company, friends."

When she saw that several others were going to speak up, she stopped them.

"You," she said to Elyara, "are welcome to come. But I would ask that you see Y'arren first lest she has need of you."

"You two," she said to Bristol and Dagna, "need to return to the imperial capital with Nerthus and prepare the way for the Alfar."

"You, Madame Directorate," she said, addressing Maeva with her future formal title for the first time, "must keep your promise to me, and your vow to Talan."

"We'll negotiate with the Empire in good faith," Maeva said with a slight bow.

"And you," Raine said, addressing the Ha'kan, and specifically Gimle, "must assist Idonea in preparing Skye. You," she said turning to Senta, "must prepare the Ha'kan for war. And you," she said, turning to the High Priestess, "must make your people very happy so they fight well."

Astrid smiled her sultry smile. "Consider it done."

Raine turned to Queen Halla. "I believe my next destination is a return to the Empire, but Talan and I have enjoyed the time we spent here. We're grateful for your hospitality."

"You're always welcome. Your chambers will be kept as is, within my forum, and we hope that you consider this a home for you."

"I'm honored, and will do so."

CHAPTER 11

The Alfar procession was leaving, and Raine decided to accompany them to the far outskirts of the capital province. Feyden and Lorifal joined her, as did Dallan, Rika, and Skye. They all rode easily on horseback, and Skye, who was masterful on a horse, thought Raine rode like a centaur. They chatted comfortably on the way, the tone decidedly different than weeks earlier when the Alfar had arrived.

"Might I try your bow someday?" Skye asked Raine.

"Of course," Raine said, "it's very dangerous, so I'll have to show you how to do it."

Feyden leaned over. He liked the slender Tavinter very much. "She makes it look easy, but I can tell you from experience, it's nearly impossible to handle."

Skye's eyes glowed at the prospective challenge.

"I tried it once," Feyden continued, "and nearly amputated a finger."

"More like an arm," Lorifal reminded him, breaking into laughter.

Raine felt good. Despite the assassination attempt and the involvement of the Shadow Guild and possibly the dragons, events seemed to be coming together. She felt more optimistic than she had in some time.

They reached the border all too soon, and Raine said farewell to Maeva and Kiren, promising to see them within weeks in the imperial capital. The much smaller band watched the Alfar procession leave, allowing their horses to forage in the tall grass. A nearby stream beckoned, and Raine kneeled down to scoop the clear running water to get a drink. She stood upright, looking out across the countryside. The sky was azure blue, the sun was a warm, buttery yellow, the grass was an endless field of bright green, and the branches of the trees moved gently in the warm wind.

And suddenly, Raine was bitterly cold. A chill enveloped her. She froze in place, looking to the others who now gazed at her in fear and horror.

"R-Raine?" Skye said, trembling.

"I know," Raine said, resignation in her voice. She turned around and looked up.

A woman towered over her, a woman dressed completely in black, the darkness a stark contrast to her alabaster skin. That ebony paled in comparison to the darkness that swirled about her and came off her body in smoky wisps. Her sumptuous, arcane garb did not end at the ground but rather joined with it, as if the woman had risen from the earth itself. The dark robes were layered and draped her voluptuous body, accentuating the paleness of the perfect cleavage thrust in Raine's face. She wore an elaborate, horned headdress that framed beautiful and cruel features. Emerald green eyes both glittered and smoldered in an unholy paradox that was further perpetuated by her cold yet volcanic expression. Blood-red lips glistened as they parted to breathe out her words.

"Hello, my love."

Raine was terrified, not only for herself, but her friends. There was nothing she could do against the being in front of her. She was immune to magic, but the gods did not need magic to force their will upon mortals, and she could not move. Every Scinterian marking on her body came to life and rose to the surface in a defensive reaction.

Hel placed her hands on Raine's hips and pulled her close, breathing in her scent. She ran her fingertips over the blue and gold markings on the muscular arms, examining them with pleasure. Raine closed her eyes, fighting the sensations that shot through her like lighting, but it was of no use. When she re-opened her eyes, they were a deep violet. Hel saw the response and pressed Raine's head to the cushion of her breasts.

"I missed you, my little Arlanian," she whispered, her voice as cold as the grave.

Skye made a small move toward them, but Feyden restrained her as Raine cried out.

"Don't."

Hel's smoldering gaze flicked up to the small band, then dismissed them, returning to her captured prey. She could not have been less interested in the others present. That was a mistake.

"Take your hands off her."

Hel smiled and turned to the stunning creature clothed from head to toe in wicked dragonscale armor that danced with flames.

"Talan," Hel said, with both sarcasm and pleasure. She examined the dragon languorously. "I missed you, too."

"But I just saw you a few weeks ago, in the palace courtyard," Talan reminded her.

"Ah," Hel replied, "but I didn't get a chance to 'see' you because you came up behind me. But if I remember correctly, that's the way you like it."

Talan ignored the suggestive, biting comment. Encouraging that conversation would cause the volcano to erupt.

"You may not take her from this realm. You know that."

"Hmm," Hel replied, as if it were no matter. She brushed Raine's hair from her eyes.

"Not even you will disobey the Allfather," Talan warned.

The glittering emerald eyes came up at the words.

"Not yet," Hel said in a hard tone. She returned to her captive and brushed the back of her hand on Raine's cheek. A muscle in Talan's jaw twitched at the caress, but she remained silent and still.

"I didn't come to retrieve her; I'll wait for her to come to me." Hel took Raine's chin in her hand and gently forced her to look up. She lowered her head and her lips hovered close to Raine's, and Talan did not know if she could restrain herself if Hel kissed her.

But Hel did not deliver the kiss but drew back, and Raine's relief was enormous. But within the relief, there was a small degree of disappointment and longing that dismayed and disgusted her. Hel saw all of these emotions and smiled her icy smile.

"It will be soon."

"I will not come to you," Raine said through clenched teeth.

"Ah," Hel said with certainty, "but you will."

Hel released her and Raine staggered and went to her knees. Talan took a step forward then stopped herself. Hel examined the fallen Arlanian.

"I think I like you in that position."

Raine's rage gave her strength and courage. She leaped to her feet to charge the Goddess, but Hel stopped her with the raise of a hand. Raine was once again immobilized, jolted to a stand-still. Talan feared for her young lover, for Hel viewed any resistance as sacrilege. But the Goddess was merely entertained and possibly even aroused by the display of anger.

"You're going to be fun," she said with that same air of inevitability.

Hel released her and Raine again fell to her knees, for any touch by the Goddess, direct or indirect, was draining. Hel gave the Arlanian one last searing look, then turned to Talan.

"Thank you for a wonderful visit. It was a perfect distraction."

And then Hel was gone. Weynild rushed to Raine's side and picked her upright as if she weighed nothing. Raine's legs buckled, but Weynild held her so she would not fall, pressing her close. Raine's skin was ice-cold, and her teeth chattered as she struggled to get a sentence out.

"What—, what did she mean? About the distraction?"

"Skye?"

Dallan was looking about her, growing concerned. Rika joined her.

"Skye!" Rika called out, louder.

Lorifal drew his axe, but Feyden shook his head, his expression somber. The two Ha'kan began combing the brush frantically, looking for their comrade.

"Skye!"

Raine stared in disbelief, still held upright by Weynild. "She took her," Raine said numbly, "she took her right in front of us."

Weynild returned to the Ha'kan capital in dragon form with Raine on her back. She came in at great speed but landed as gently as possible. Queen Halla watched with concern as the dragon lowered her head and Raine stumbled from the serpentine neck, falling to the terrace. Senta ran over as Weynild transformed. The First General helped Raine to her feet, half holding her until Weynild joined and put her arm about Raine's waist, supporting her entire weight.

"What's happened?" Halla exclaimed.

"The Alfar?" Senta asked, feeling dread.

"No," Raine said, "the Alfar are safe and on their way. But—,"

Raine was overcome with grief and anger, and Weynild had to finish for her.

"Hel came in the forest, to torture my love again."

Raine shook her head. “She came as a distraction.”

“A distraction?” Senta asked. “For what?”

“She took Skye!”

Halla gasped and put her hand to her breast. Astrid placed her hand upon the Queen’s shoulder to comfort her, but she too was overcome.

“Your daughter is safe,” Weynild said, answering the unasked question, “As are all others but Skye. Even now they ride like the Valkyries to get back here. They’ll join us in the meeting hall.”

It was a far smaller group that met in the amphitheater this time. There were no Alfar, other than Feyden, far fewer Ha’kan, and only a handful of imperials. Dallan’s agitation was evident and Halla sought to soothe her daughter, as did Lifa. Torsten appeared, having heard word, and he was brought in as Skye’s second-in-command and oldest friend. The grief of the Ha’kan and Tavinter was enormous, surpassed only by that of Raine’s. Her fury was barely contained within the frame that shook from cold and the anger that seethed within her.

“I’ll go after her,” she said. “This is because of me.”

“You and Skye are much alike,” came the ancient, wizened voice, “always taking the blame for things that aren’t your fault.”

Raine looked up in surprise, as did all. A very old man in a wizard’s robe embroidered with arcane symbols older than time was being escorted into the room. He moved slowly, supporting himself on his staff and the arm of Elyara.

“Isleif,” Raine said, disbelief in her voice.

“In the flesh,” he said, sighing. “For a while longer.”

“I must go after her!” Raine insisted. “The filament I created still connects us. I’ll be able to find her.”

"The filament is exactly why you must not go," Isleif said.

"Isleif is right," Weynild said. "This is a trap. Hel must know of the bond."

"She might not," Raine argued, "she might just see Skye as a future threat."

"The gods don't fear magic," Isleif said.

For a long moment Raine looked at Weynild and some silent communication passed between them.

"They should," Raine said at last.

"Hel didn't kill Skye," Isleif continued, "so she can't take her from this realm. My guess is that Ingrid has Skye, captured with Hel's assistance in order to lay a trap for you."

"I can handle that sorceress," Raine said.

"You're not listening, my love," Weynild said gently but firmly. "It's a trap. One set specifically for you."

"You can't sacrifice yourself, not even for my great-granddaughter," Isleif said. "The prophecy must be fulfilled."

"What prophecy is that?" Gimle asked. She had studied the history of Arianthem extensively and never heard of such a thing.

"It's old," Isleif explained, "far older than anyone in this room, pre-dating even the Queen of Dragons," he said with a respectful nod towards Weynild. "No one understood it. But when Raine and Talan found one another, both I and the elven seer Y'arren began to think it referred to Raine. Time has only strengthened that belief."

"What does the prophecy say?" Halla asked.

"In simple terms, it states that when the end of the world approaches, only the Dragon's Lover stands between life and total destruction. The words are written in a very obscure version of ancient Elvish, but the accepted translation is 'the Dragon's Lover, felled by the closest of allies, carries into death without dying that which saves all worlds.' There is a final line to the poem, but no one has been able to translate it."

"So, you expect me to do nothing?" Raine demanded.

"We'll go for her," Dallan spoke up.

"Yes," Senta agreed, putting her hand on Dallan's shoulder, "the Ha'kan will search for Skye."

"Very noble of you," Isleif said, "and appreciated. But I've been preparing for this since Skye was born." He turned his bushy eyebrows toward Idonea. "Will you do this for me, my dear?"

"Of course, love," Idonea said, as if she were agreeing to go for stroll, "it sounds like fun."

Isleif pulled a small vial from inside his cloak. "I took this from Skye when she was an infant." The red liquid swirled about in the tiny glass container. "In the event the magic was in her blood. You can find her with it."

Idonea took the vial and hooked it to the chain on her belt, then tucked it safely into her pocket.

"We'll accompany you," Dallan said, "and bring whatever force you wish."

"I'll go, too."

The Lady Jorden glanced to her companion in surprise. Syn had been utterly quiet in all previous proceedings and had spent the entire time in the capital trying to remain unnoticed, typical of a master thief. But now she spoke up.

"I faced the sorceress with Skye before," Syn said, "and I'll gladly do so again."

"Better be careful," Raine said with approval, "you're in danger of becoming respectable."

"Well, that's not going to happen," Syn said, "but Skye and the Tavinter have taken me in like family. I owe her."

"And I have a few resources I can bring to the table," Jorden said, "in all these matters."

"I'll join you," Nerthus said to Idonea, "as soon as I'm finished with the Emperor."

"Mmm," Idonea said.

"So, we're agreed," Weynild said in summary. "I'll go seek out my kind. You," she said to Raine, "will seek out the assassins. And you, my beloved daughter, will find Skye."

CHAPTER 12

Ingrid watched the girl in her bed. That Tavinter had only grown more beautiful with time. Blonde hair curled about angelic features. Long dark eyelashes fluttered against a tan, sun-kissed cheek, and Ingrid leaned forward, thinking she was about to awaken. She did not, and the sorceress sat back, resuming her vigil.

She glanced to herself in the mirror. She was vain beyond measure, but that vanity was vindicated by the reflection that stared back at her. Pale, perfect skin, long white hair, striking blue eyes, full red lips that could reveal the inner ugliness when curled in scorn. But she could hide that ugliness and was practiced at doing so. The lips turned into a relaxed smile and the expression on the face became one of gentle, loving concern.

What had that demon told her, the messenger of the Goddess? "She will be delivered to you with her mind wiped clean. She will remember nothing. You may fill that emptiness as you wish, but take care not to stir the past."

And Ingrid had taken great care. They were in a castle in the remotest of lands, with nothing to remind the Tavinter of who she was. Her leather armor had been removed and destroyed; now she wore silken clothes befitting a noblewoman. All her weapons had been disposed of, replaced with the tools of leisure and aristocracy: books, parchments, quills, and musical instruments. There was nothing in the castle to remind the girl of the harsh, nomadic life she had lived, nothing to remind her of the days with the Ha'kan, and plenty to reinforce the illusion she was simply the young lover of a wealthy imperial landowner.

The girl stirred again, and this time the hazel eyes fluttered open, unfocused. Ingrid placed a cold compress on her forehead.

"Be still, my love, you've taken a terrible blow to the head. I never should have let you get on that horse. You're so fragile."

The girl looked at the lovely woman leaning over her and was deeply confused. She did not know her. She looked around the room and nothing looked familiar. Even more confusing, she could not seem to remember her own name, or really anything about herself.

"Could I, could I have a drink of water?" Skye whispered.

"Of course, my love. Here you are."

The woman leaned over her and lifted Skye's head gently to help her drink. As she did so, her full breasts pressed against Skye. The cool water felt wonderful on her parched, swollen tongue, and the view of those superb, round mounds of flesh was the first thing that was close to familiar to Skye. She flushed, uncertain if her gaze was inappropriate or expected. The woman had called her "my love," but she could not be sure what that meant.

Ingrid watched closely for any fear or recognition that would betray her ruse and saw nothing. The girl displayed only hesitant uncertainty. When Ingrid saw the eyes tentatively settle on her breasts, she saw her first opportunity to reinforce the "relationship" she had created.

"The doctor said you might have trouble remembering things," Ingrid said. She leaned down and kissed the feverish brow, allowing another generous view of her breasts. "Does this help you remember?"

Skye felt a stirring in her loins and sincerely hoped this was not her mother. The woman disabused that notion by trailing her kiss down the flushed cheek, then kissing her fully on the lips. The kiss was gentle at first, the lips soft on hers, and it felt pleasingly familiar to Skye. The kiss deepened and the stirring in Skye increased: this was most definitely not her mother. A hand brushed between her legs, a light stroke that elicited a soft moan from Skye.

Ingrid fought to control her excitement. The girl's ready response told her she remembered nothing. She withdrew the hands and lips, pleased to see the longing in those hazel eyes.

"I'm so sorry, my dear, it's far too soon. But I've so missed you. My bed has been so empty without you!"

"I'm sure I'll be better soon," Skye said uncertainly. She was embarrassed she could remember nothing when this woman so obviously loved her.

"I've waited so long," Ingrid said, successfully suppressing the note of triumph in her voice. "I can wait a little longer."

CHAPTER 13

The chambers of the Goddess of the Underworld were almost as dreadful as their inhabitant. Ebony surfaces gleamed, lit red by fire that flickered and twisted as if in pain. Blood-red candles by the hundreds bled crimson wax that dripped into distorted and horrific formations. A huge bed, its frame of hardened lava, rose up from the flooring in a roughly rectangular formation. The bed was a stark contrast to its rough jagged frame, obscenely soft, lined with black silken sheets and black silken pillows. And the Queen of the Underworld's skin was a stark contrast to those black sheets as she lay on her back gazing up at the high vaulted ceiling that perennially mimicked the night sky. Her nipples hardened and reached toward that sky as a minion dutifully serviced her between her legs.

Her thoughts wandered idly as the wickedly long tongue of her thrall did its business. This last little foray into the worldly realm had been a great success. She cared nothing for the petty machinations of mortals, or even for the more grandiose maneuverings of the dragons. They were all small to her. The armies of the Underworld, when ready, would defeat them all.

The trap had been set for the Arlanian, but Hel doubted that Talan would be so foolish to allow her love to walk into it. No, that had not really been the purpose of any of that. Rather, that had been just a distraction, another feint, another step closer to her ultimate goal.

Talan had once again passed through Nifelheim to save her lover. Hel had felt the dragon's presence, even been able to faintly detect her progress this time. The next time Talan entered her realm, that shadowy curtain between both worlds that belonged to the Goddess of the Dead, Hel would be waiting.

This thought pleasantly occupied Hel's dark thoughts as the throbbing pressure between her legs increased, brought on by the skilled exertions of her thrall. And she had one last thought before her body released: soon it would be that Arlanian kneeling between her legs bringing her to climax. This image was enough to push her over the edge as endless waves of pleasure overcame her.

Chapter 14

Weynild was wrapped tightly about Raine. Raine's body had warmed once again, aided by the enormous fire in the fireplace but even more so by the hours of lovemaking that had preceded their now quiet embrace.

"See," Raine said, "I was right. Our previous period of abstinence merely delayed my recovery."

"Yes, you were right," Weynild said, stroking her hair. Even in Raine's fatigued condition, their sex was passionate and prolonged, if a bit melancholy.

Raine was quiet and Weynild thought she had gone to sleep. She had not.

"Do you think Isleif is right? That Skye's with that sorceress?"

"I do," Weynild said.

"Do you think she'll hurt her?"

Weynild spoke after some thought. "No, although I'm not sure how the sorceress plans to contain her. Skye is very powerful, but still unaware. Somehow the sorceress must maintain that unawareness."

"I'm going to kill Ingrid one day," Raine said.

"Not if the Ha'kan get to her first," Weynild said, "or Idonea."

The thought that Idonea went forward without her troubled Raine. "Idonea's gifts are without measure, but can she defeat Ingrid if she's aided by Hel?"

"It won't be easy," Weynild admitted, "but I have faith in my daughter."

Raine again grew quiet and her breathing deepened. Her mind was still unsettled, and she sought to dwell on more pleasant things, even those that were impossible. The pleasing impossibilities somewhat eased her morose mood and she shared them drowsily.

"Your children are a handful. Can you imagine what ours would be like if we could have them?"

This elicited the low, throaty chuckle from her love that Raine adored.

"By the Divine, no," Weynild said. "But a half-dragon, Arlanian-Scinterian would rule the world through charm alone. I would only hope that the child would inherit your appetites and not mine, or every creature in Arianthem would be in danger."

"Yes," Raine said, savoring this most wonderful thought as she drifted off to sleep, "but they would all enjoy it."

Also by Samantha

Scan to see the series!

THE CHRONICLES OF ARIANTHEM

THE DRAGON'S LOVER (Book 1)
THE SJÖFN ACADEMY (Book 2)
THE RUNNER THIEF (Book 3)
THE RIVAL'S CONCORD (Book 4)
THE DRAGON'S ALLIANCE (Book 5)
THE SHADOW GAMES (Book 6)
THE DRAGON'S WAR (Book 7)
THE GODDESS OF THE UNDERWORLD (Book 8)

2nd CHRONICLES OF ARIANTHEM

THE DRAGON'S NIGHT (Book 9)
THE SCINTERIAN'S DREAM (Book 10)
THE RISE OF THE SINISTER (Book 11)

About the Author

Samantha Sabian, author of the "Chronicles of Arianthem" series, enjoys writing about strong, sexy women. Not content simply to tell stories, she creates *worlds*. Her irreverent sense of humor often spills out of the mouths of her characters, who come alive in these remarkable fantasy settings.

Samantha lives in Southern California where she happily spends her day working out, attending art school, and of course, writing. She lives with a cacophony of parrots (more appropriate than "flock"), whose personalities find their way into her books, usually in the form of bossy little dragons.

Samantha tries to answer all email, so drop her a note:

Samantha@arianthem.com

www.ingramcontent.com/pod-product-compliance
Lightning Source LLC
Chambersburg PA
CBHW072106170626
46813CB00004B/1477
9780988582286